— CALE'S STORY —

— CALE'S STORY —

A Novel by
KEVIN J. ANDERSON &
REBECCA MOESTA

ACE BOOKS, NEW YORK

TITAN A.E.™: CALE'S STORY

An Ace Book / published by arrangement with
Twentieth Century Fox Animation

PRINTING HISTORY
Ace edition / May 2000

The Penguin Putnam Inc. World Wide Web site address is
http://www.penguinputnam.com

Check out the ACE Science Fiction & Fantasy newsletter
and much more on the Internet at Club PPI!

ISBN: 0-441-00737-6

ACE®
Ace Books are published
by The Berkley Publishing Group,
a division of Penguin Putnam Inc.,
375 Hudson Street, New York, New York 10014.
ACE and the "A" design are trademarks
belonging to Penguin Putnam Inc.

PRINTED IN THE UNITED STATES OF AMERICA

10 9 8 7 6 5 4 3 2 1

— ACKNOWLEDGMENTS —

Special thanks to many people.

Ginjer Buchanan from Ace Books: for choosing to work with us on yet another fun book project.

Virginia King, Melissa Cobb, and Jennifer Robinson from Fox: for your faith in us, and for listening to our ideas.

Matt Bialer of the William Morris Agency: for convincing us this would be an entertaining and worthwhile project.

Catherine Sidor and Diane E. Jones from WordFire, Inc.: for all the hours and effort you put in to help us finish this book and make it as good as it could be.

Jonathan MacGregor Cowan: for putting up with weeks and months of "Not right now." "Can it wait?" "I'm almost done." And so on.

— ABOUT THE AUTHORS —

Kevin J. Anderson and Rebecca Moesta (a husband-and-wife writing team) have written two dozen books together, and dozens more separately. For more information on their works, please visit them on the web at www.wordfire.com or www.dunenovels.com, or write to them care of

AnderZone
P.O. Box 767
Monument, CO 80132-0767

— 1 —

The Earth had been destroyed . . . but he had to admit, this place didn't look much better. Cale Tucker did not have good luck in picking planets to call home.

Generations of heavy-duty industrialism had used up the world of Vusstra, and all that remained was a grayish, tired landscape. The natives here survived only by taking off-world commissions, processing materials brought in by orbital cargo haulers, and then doing the work on the surface. The Vusstrans used creaking, age-old facilities, many of which had already been abandoned like rusty dinosaur skeletons in deserted valleys.

And Tek claims this place used to be green and lush and beautiful, Cale thought, scratching his straw-blond hair as he surveyed the desolation. Cale's alien guardian, Tek, claimed that Vusstra had once teemed with life. But then, this place was Tek's home, and he probably let his pride interfere with his eyesight (and his common sense).

After spending most of his childhood here—ten Earth

years, or twelve Vusstran cycles—Cale had seen everything worth looking at on Vusstra. In fact, it had taken more like ten or twelve *minutes*.

At least he didn't have to go far to feel completely alone, where he could brood in peace. Less than an hour's walk from the cluster of rounded dwellings in the dying industrial city where he lived with Tek, Cale could find himself in an utter wasteland.

If Tek's proud imaginings could be believed, this broad valley had once been a paradise, with a running stream, meadow flowers, and wildlife. Now the valley floor could barely support the sparse, scrubby vegetation that surrounded its thermal hot springs and mudpots; rusted girders and derricks were the only remnants of long-bankrupt processing facilities.

Cale often took advantage of the solitude. Now, he sat on a large, sharp rock at the edge of the bubbling mud pools. He stared into the roiling paste of brown and green and gray—a fitting reflection of his own simmering emotions, bubbling up from inside.

He'd been stuck on this planet ever since the evil alien Drej had chosen Earth as their next target for destruction. Despite the warnings, despite the best efforts of Human defense forces, the implacable, unstoppable Drej had blown up the Earth. Cale and millions of refugees—only a small fraction of the doomed population—had escaped at the last moment, taking any functional ship they could find.

Tek, the genial Vusstran who'd worked with Cale's father for years on the Titan Project, had taken the young boy under his wing. Now, though, as he looked around himself and thought of his life after Earth, Cale wasn't sure how much of a favor that had been. . . .

Lines of rugged, cinnamon-colored mountains encircled the bowl of the valley. As the sun slipped down into afternoon, shadows highlighted clefts in the rock like zebra stripes. A few hardy plants poked up between algae-covered boulders, and some stubble and meager brush ringed the mudpots. The plants were tough and brittle, though, more thorns than leaves, enough to discourage even the hungriest of grazing animals.

The sky overhead, a drab olive-green smeared with beige, was murky from smoke and exhausts that had filled the air of Vusstra for centuries. Sharp-winged birds, little more than checkmarks, cruised so high up that they could see the entire valley, searching with intense eyesight for any small prey. As far as Cale could tell, they had been circling there for a long time. By now, they must be very hungry.

He shifted on the rough-edged rock. A particularly large bubble in the mudpot popped with a rude noise and sprayed an odor of brimstone in his face. Tek claimed that bathing in the warm mud was healthy for the hide, but when Cale had tried it, it seemed to take weeks to get all of the grit out of his pores.

Now he fixed his green-eyed stare on the muddy scenery, complaining to himself because no one else would bother to listen. He resented being stranded here and resented even more that his father had not come back for him as he'd promised.

Just before the aliens had blown up Earth, Sam Tucker had separated from his son. Unceremoniously, he'd dumped the five-year-old boy into the waiting arms of Tek, extracted a promise from the Vusstran scientist, and then raced off into the immense technological facility, hidden under an innocuous-looking barn in farm country.

"Cale, I have to go on a different ship. I have to go away for awhile," he had said. Just about the last words he'd ever heard his father speak.

But how much longer than ten years was "awhile"? What good was it when you couldn't even trust your father to keep his promises? What kind of life was it to grow up here on this scab of a planet? Cale snorted and kicked a rock into the mudpool, where it splashed, then sank with a loud *bloop*.

Supposedly, the Titan Project held the hope of Earth and the secret for mankind's eventual return to glory. *Supposedly*.

Despite Tek's grandiose dreams, Cale knew that Vusstra was a washed-out old place, stripped bare and exploited for too many centuries. The Vusstrans had expanded through the galaxy, setting up outposts, living on space stations and mining colonies. But as they continued their commerce across the Spiral Arm, the Vusstrans had hardly noticed how depleted the natural resources were on their own world. Now Tek, using much of Sam Tucker's research about sparking life on other worlds, hoped that he could do the same with his own lethargic planet.

As if even Tek could believe all the things Sam Tucker had told him. . . .

Cale looked down at the gold ring on his finger, an intricately scribed piece of jewelry that his father had given him just before rushing off. "I want you to always keep this. I will see you again."

As a young boy, Cale had been absorbed in tinkering with his own gadgets, proud of each minor success that he could show his father, who was working on bigger and more extravagant inventions. Cale's mother had died when he was only three. She had worn a ring, but not this one. And he'd never noticed this ring on his father's finger, didn't know where it had come from. Yet Sam Tucker had been most insistent that Cale take it and wear it.

Now with the mudpot steaming and bubbling in front of him, Cale angrily twisted the ring on his finger. *Always keep this.* He wondered uncharitably if the older man had just given the ring as an impromptu token, so that his little boy would think he'd planned ahead for their painful separation. *I will see you again.*

Growling under his breath, Cale yanked the ring off his finger. This was the only thing he had left of his father, the only tangible memory of Earth. But what did it matter? What good did some trinket do, some piece of junk that his father had jammed on his finger? Did it mean anything at all? He doubted it. Cale would much rather have his father back, his old life back—all of it, including Earth.

Cale flicked his wrist and impulsively tossed the ring into the thick, sulfurous mud. The ring spun in the air, glittering under the dim olive sky, then plopped into the runny, smelly substance, where it would soon sink and vanish. Forever.

"Awww," he groaned with a pang of regret. He still didn't want to get rid of the ring entirely. *I want you to always keep this.* Despite his anger, he slid off the big rock and knelt at the edge of the mudpot. Heat from the

warm mud penetrated the knees of his dark hiking jump-
suit. The ring was starting to sink in the thick, warm
mud. Holding on to the rock with one hand, he leaned
out over the mud and stuck his other hand into the hot
goop, trying to reach the ring, but he couldn't stretch far
enough. Mud covered his sleeve up to the elbow.

From a warren in the far side of the pit, a muskrat-
sized creature peered out with three sparkling eyes and
a twitching nose. It watched Cale. Then it saw the ring,
the beautiful golden ring, and ignored the big Human
entirely. The creature had long, thick strands of gray-
blue fur and a callused black snout that wrinkled at the
sharp rotten-egg smell. It made its move, skittering
across the squishy surface, walking on wide, webbed
feet. Shaped like paddles, the feet helped it keep its balance as it dodged the bubbles.

The ring disappeared below the muddy surface.

Cale leaned one more time into the mire, stroking outward until his arm was covered in mud up to the shoulders, but he still couldn't reach the ring. "Come on!"

The packrodent darted in front of him at a waddling
run. With astonishing speed, it plunged beneath the mud,
like an otter after a fish, wallowing and squirming until
it came up with the ring clenched in its buck teeth.

Cale jumped to his feet. "Hey! You put that down."

The creature chittered at him.

Casting common sense aside, Cale lunged for the ring,
leaning far out over the mudpot. "Give it back!" Just
then, the crusty soil on the lip of the pit crumbled, and
he plunged face-first into the bubbling, stinking mud.
"Ow!" he yelled, more startled than burned.

Cale splashed around, trying to regain his balance, but

only succeeded in sinking waist-deep into the muck.
Ashy mud coated his eyes and nose and mouth. He
wiped at it with one hand, redistributing the goo but not
removing any.

Cale lunged again, but the packrodent slipped away
with a strangely balanced waddle-gallop as it skittered
across the viscous muck to its warren in the soft bank.

"Come back here!" Cale waded through the thick ooze
until he fell again, sideways this time, getting the smelly
muck caked into the rest of his blond hair. His pride hurt
more than the hot mud did. Forgoing all caution now,
he scrambled forward just as the creature disappeared
into the hole of its den.

Without hesitation, his anger making him even more
impulsive than usual, Cale reached in. "That's *my* ring!"
He grabbed the rodent's tail, but the matted fur was too
slippery with mud for him to keep his grip.

Fuming, Cale backed off and began to tear open the
mud-walled burrow with his bare hands. He cracked his
fingernails and scraped his hands raw widening the den
opening so that he could reach deeper inside. He shoved
his arm in up to his shoulder, patting with his hand and
wiggling his fingers. There, his fingertips found smooth,
rounded things. He grabbed one of the objects and
snatched it out. His triumph was short-lived. It was only
a glittery fossil shell the creature had found somewhere.

"Where's my ring?" He dug deeper into the warren.
The packrodent nipped at his fingers, and Cale jerked
his hand back, this time clutching a metal jar lid from
some long-abandoned mine office.

Annoyed, Cale threw it over his shoulder into the
mud.

"Hey, Cale—you're a home wrecker!" a high-pitched voice said. And then a truly annoying giggle echoed from above the mudpots.

Entirely covered with muck, Cale looked up. His eyes were the only clean part of his body. Even so, every time he blinked, bits of dirt blurred his vision.

Iji, Tek's young pod-daughter, sat there, her round, greenish-brown face crinkled with mirth, her snout's overhanging lip curled in a grin that stretched from ear hole to ear hole. Iji's round eyes blinked like a predatory fish. While fatherly Tek insisted that Iji was insufferably cute for a young girl of her species, Cale just found her to be a pest.

"That critter stole my ring," he said defensively, and dug around inside again, pulling out more trinkets and treasures the packrodent had stashed away. Disgusted, he tossed them into the bubbling mud behind him and dug the hole wider. Finally his hand closed around the ring, and he pulled it out.

Grinning, he held it up. "See. I got it back."

Half a second later the creature lunged out at him like a wet-furred bullet. The packrodent struck him full in the face, pushing him backward as it tried to escape. Cale fell down into the mudpot again, fingers clenched around the ring. He spat out a mouthful of the hot dirt, flailing and thrashing as the packrodent strode on its webbed feet across his face and walked indignantly into the goop to begin retrieving its stolen treasures.

Cale came up spluttering, sloshed to the side of the mudpot, and climbed out onto solid ground.

Iji sat giggling on a dirt ridge above him. "You'd better get back home before all that mud dries on you," she said, without moving a single, spotted hand to help him. "Otherwise we'll have a new statue for the front yard." Her nose slits flared. "But I don't think Father would want anything that ugly for a yard ornament."

"I'm not the one who's ugly, you *Ijit*," Cale said, using his scornful pet name for the little girl. He jammed the ring back onto his muddy finger and climbed up out of the basin. The cloudy, olive skies were threatening rain, and the air had grown uncomfortably cool. It would be a long, long trudge back to the dwellings.

— 2 —

By the time he approached Tek's rounded, cermet house, Cale was weary, wet, chilled to the core, and annoyed—mostly with himself. The constant drizzle from the smear of low greenish clouds had kept the mud moist and unpleasant. The sulfurous dirt caked on him smelled strongly enough that he didn't notice the usual bitter stink of pollution in the air of Vusstra.

In sharp contrast to the planet's dinginess and pollution, the walls of Vusstran dwellings were made of a creamy translucent ceramic-and-metal alloy that was elegant, energy-efficient, and easy to keep clean. The luminous towers of their house seemed to beckon Cale, promising welcome and warmth. He quickened his pace.

Iji had pestered him every step of the way back to the settlement, and he ignored her, as usual. He had spent the long walk turning the ring on his finger around and around, wondering first what had possessed him to throw his father's ring away, and then what inner demon had driven him to retrieve it. The thoughts circling in his mind chafed as much as the ring twisting on his finger.

Tek met him at the door to their four-story home with a curious and watchful expression, as if he knew he'd never understand the quirks of Humans. "Cale, you'll have to clean up before coming inside. But don't waste too much water." Hovering in the doorway, Tek glanced back into their house, no doubt anxious to return to his work.

The wind was picking up, and the wan sunlight that penetrated the thick clouds provided little warmth, but Cale took the news with stoic resignation. Cold as he was already, he couldn't blame his alien foster father. After all, the thin drizzle of rain had only served to thin the volcanic mud that covered Cale from head to toe and allow it to sink more deeply into his clothing.

What did irritate Cale, however, was that Iji sneaked up behind him seconds later with a bucket from the reclaimed-water cistern and dumped it over his head. He spluttered, feeling the shock of the frigid splash. Wiping the water from his eyes with numb fingers, Cale looked over at Tek to see if he would intercede.

The older Vusstran's long, rounded snout twitched with amusement. "Hmmm, yes. Much better now. Less mud."

Cale growled, shaking moisture from his hair as the waterlogged packrodent had done. He rounded on his pod-sister with a look of gleeful menace. "You just wait, little Ijit. You're going to pay for that—when you least expect it."

Just then, the rain unexpectedly changed from a mere drizzle to an outright downpour. Iji squealed and ducked into the entryway of the house, where Tek had already piled several ragged towels from his collection.

With a shrug and a resigned sigh, Cale stayed where he was for several minutes and let the rain wash him clean.

After supper, Tek watched his pod-daughter and Cale place the dishes and the remains of their evening meal into the recyclemat. Inside the machine, every scrap of material would be analyzed, then either cleaned or recycled for use in another form. On depleted, resource-poor Vusstra, wastefulness of any sort was not tolerated.

Tek's round eyes twinkled with good humor as he watched the two gibe and bicker just as if they were actual siblings. Perhaps this was not surprising since they had been raised together for more than ten Vusstran cycles. Yet the two had come into Tek's care in such different ways.

In the final days of the Titan Project, before the Drej had destroyed Earth, Cale's father, Sam Tucker, had extracted a promise from Tek: a promise to care for the boy and keep him safe from the Drej until Sam Tucker himself—or one of his trusted Human colleagues—could return and take over Cale's upbringing. Because Tucker and Tek had been both friends and kindred spirits, Tek had readily agreed.

And so, after the end of Earth, Tek had returned to Vusstra and raised young Cale Tucker as his foster son. Ryt, Tek's wife, had accepted the Human boy without question. She had been close to Cale's mother before the Earth woman had died two years earlier, and Ryt herself had been unable to produce children—not an unusual circumstance on the polluted world. For Ryt and Tek, Cale had filled an empty place in their lives.

At the thought of his beloved wife, Tek turned toward the translucent cermet wall to hide the sadness on his face. He pressed a stud in the curved wall to activate the magnetic field. As the field shifted, an area of the cermet wall changed from translucent to transparent, and Tek studied the view through the window. His jowly face sagged with emotion.

While Cale's arrival had been a blessing, Iji herself had been a miracle. Iji's parents had been killed in a transport accident at one of Vusstra's major industrial plants where Ryt had been taking some environmental samples for analysis. When the pregnant Vusstran woman died, the pod she'd carried had been expected to die as well. But Ryt had taken over nurturing the pod, and—to everyone's surprise—the child, Iji, had lived.

Outside the window, the blanket of brownish clouds began to break up.

Young as he was, Cale had helped care for Iji from the moment the pod had cracked open. The four of them had become a family of sorts, closer because of the strange circumstances that had brought them together. Even Ryt's death three years ago (from a disorder caused by the environmental pollutants she'd been studying) had not been able to tear their little family apart. Tek, Iji, and Cale relied on one another more than ever now. Ryt would have been proud of them.

As darkness fell, the sky cleared enough for faint twinkling stars to shine through. Ryt had loved the stars, although a veil of smog covered them nineteen nights out of twenty. Tonight, though, the unexpected downpour had washed the skies clean. Gazing at the stars together was one of their most cherished family traditions. Tek turned away from the window and looked at Cale and Iji. With a twitch of his beaklike snout, he said. "The stars are out. First one to the rooftop can use my astrascope."

Cale and Iji scrambled for the stairs.

Up on the flat rooftop gallery of the dwelling, Cale picked mud from under his fingernails while he waited for his turn with Tek's astrascope. The air still had an unpleasant chemical tang, but it was an unusually clear night. Even without the help of the instrument, Cale could see more stars than he remembered seeing since, since. . . .

His memories of Earth were faint. Cale still had vague images of times with his father, when Sam Tucker wasn't consumed all day and all night with his work on Titan. More clearly, Cale remembered *leaving* the man, remembered Tek taking him into a refugee spaceship and strapping him in . . . hurtling upward into a blue sky that gradually deepened to purple. Through the window-port, he'd seen another huge, round ship blasting off—the *Titan*, Tek had told him. His father's grand project, the dream, the hope of Earth. . . .

Then Cale remembered seeing his planet, so beautiful and blue with wisps of clouds, and brown and green landmasses like puzzle pieces. And the awful Drej ships, crackling electrical blue, pummeled Earth with their energy beam like a planetary jackhammer, *breaking it apart*. An explosion. Fire and rubble erupting in every direction.

Then blackness. And stars. *Billions* of stars. . . .

Cale shivered in spite of the warmth radiating from the heated cermet of the roof platform beneath him.

"Is anything wrong, Cale?" Tek asked. He looked at Cale with an odd, somber expression, as if he had seen the memories flashing through the young man's mind.

The last thing Cale wanted to do was talk about the disturbing thoughts. He shook his head. "Not really." He stepped closer to the astrascope and gave Iji a playful prod with his elbow. "Just considering how best to repay my pod-sister for that bucket of cold water earlier."

"Iji," Tek warned, "let Cale have a turn at the astrascope."

"But I won the race," Iji said, refusing to tear her eyes from the scope. "I got here first."

"You tripped me," Cale argued.

She turned up her snout at him, flaring her nostril slits—the Vusstran equivalent of sticking out her tongue.

He tweaked the scruff of her neck near a particularly sensitive patch of skin discoloration. With a squeal, she scrambled out of his way. Smiling, Cale looked into the astrascope, but his victory was tempered by a flash of uneasiness again. The sight of so many stars reminded him of his flight to Vusstra at the age of five—just after the last time he had seen his father and his planet. To divert his thoughts, he said, "Tek, tell me again about how you and my father met."

Tek leaned against the half-height wall that surrounded the circular rooftop platform. The creamy cermet material glowed with faint light and warmth. Tek placed his elbows on it and gazed up at the stars.

"It's been more than twenty cycles now since I met

Sam Tucker," Tek said. "Ryt and I were both young scientists. We met in group school, an environmental study class. Many scientists on Vusstra had given up hope for our tired world, but Ryt and I were willing to consider possibilities no one had even thought of before. We'd heard of a man on a planet named Earth. He was developing 'simple' methods of stimulating planetary ecology by using a revolutionary technique called 'bio-templating' at an elemental level."

Iji rolled her eyes, as she always did when her pod-father got more technical than he needed to in his explanations.

"That man was Sam Tucker, your father, Cale. And of course his techniques were anything but simple. Ryt and I volunteered to exchange our knowledge of environmental science and technology for a chance to assist him in the Titan Project. We hoped that we'd be able to use his ideas to rejuvenate our own world. Now that took some negotiating between the governments of Vusstra and Earth, I can tell you! We alternated our environmental work between the Titan Project and the Vusstran renewal studies."

Cale turned the astrascope, but he wasn't really paying any attention to the starry sky anymore.

"Sam Tucker and I shared many beliefs. A lot of people laughed at him, too. But he was *right*, no matter what anyone else said. We agreed on these basic things: First, a planet's future need not be determined solely by its past. Second, it is rarely too late to make a new start. Third, hope is an essential survival trait—regardless of species. And fourth, through solidarity we can accomplish almost anything. Your father had a vision for the future, Cale. He was an important man. Our spirits were very close." Tek swallowed convulsively, as if something hard and bitter had become lodged in his throat, and went silent for a long moment.

"So, where was Ryt when the Drej arrived?" Cale asked, absently twisting the ring on his finger. He didn't bother looking in the scope anymore, but did not step aside to let Iji take another turn. "And why didn't my father leave with us?"

"Ryt had just gone back to Vusstra to do data analysis when our time ran out. We were never sure why the Drej attacked so quickly, and Sam Tucker didn't know who to trust. Someone had to take the *Titan* and hide it in a safe place—to preserve it for all humankind. Your father believed he had the best chance of succeeding."

"Let's talk about something else," Iji broke in, apparently tired of being ignored. Cale didn't mind, though: he had heard enough. "Father, tell me what my name means again," she said.

Tek chuckled. "Your name in the ancient language, small one, means 'ray of light.' "

Iji's voice became sly. "And Cale's name has a meaning in the old tongue, too, doesn't it?"

Tek snorted. "You know, little daughter, that Cale was not named in our language."

Cale gritted his teeth, knowing that she was trying to irritate him. It was working. She seemed to have quite a talent for it.

"Even so." Iji's voice was filled with artificial sweetness. "Doesn't the name 'Cale' mean something?" She paused for dramatic effect. "Didn't you tell me it means . . . stable droppings?"

Later that night, she didn't even complain to Tek when she discovered—too late—that Cale had stuffed her pillow with blister-weed.

— 3 —

"**B**efore entering the research environment, all foreign contaminants must be removed or neutralized," the electronic voice said. Cale's skin began to tingle the moment he stepped into the decontamination vault. The door to the tubular chamber swished shut. The light overhead blinked, and the electronic voice instructed him to remove all garments.

"Sure, why not," he muttered darkly. "I haven't been humiliated enough in the past couple of days." Not that any Vusstran had the slightest interest in seeing naked Humans anyway.

He shed his clothes and let them drop to the floor. A small opening appeared in the chamber wall at floor level, and a pair of fist-sized scutbots trundled in on whirling sucker-tipped legs. The scutbots collected Cale's clothing and disappeared through the opening, which also vanished a moment later.

" 'Come visit the laboratory vault with me,' he says,"

Cale said in a fair imitation of Tek's voice. " 'Fabulous technology,' he says. 'Most amazing things you've ever seen in your life. It'll be fun. I guarantee you won't be bored,' " he continued muttering.

Though he tried to act nonchalant, Cale gritted his teeth as the sonic beam rattled his body, neutralizing and dislodging every possible particle of contamination. This was followed immediately by a blast of vacuum sweepers that produced a whirlwind in the tiny chamber by sucking out all particles from bottom to top, while purified filtered air was pumped through the bottom.

At the completion of the process, Cale's hair stood wildly on end. Next, light pulsated up and down the chamber walls, scanning his body. "Alert," the electronic voice said in a tone that sounded completely disinterested. "Alert. Severe physical abnormalities detected. Not standard Vusstran physiology."

"No kidding," Cale said, knowing the automated electronic voice could not pick up his sarcasm. "Do you think it could be because I'm a Human, maybe, and not a Vusstran?"

"Manual override activated," the electronic voice responded blandly. The surface beneath his feet rotated, and the chamber door swished open.

Cale found himself face-to-face with Tek, who wore a pristine white smock, along with a filternet cap on his smooth-skinned head, booties on his broad, big-nailed feet, and a mask across his beaklike snout and mouth. "Well, don't just stand there. Come in, come in. What do you think, my boy? Follow me, and we'll take a look around."

Naked and shivering, Cale cleared his throat uncom-

fortably. He saw no new set of clothes waiting for him.
When Tek did not take the hint, he said, "Uh, Tek?"

"Oh, no need to worry," Tek responded, completely
missing the point. "You're perfectly clean now. Can't
contaminate a thing. Hmm, yes. Not that the decontamination protocols weren't a bit tricky this time," he went
on, absently waving a three-fingered paw. "After all, you
are the first Human ever allowed into this laboratory. I
always wanted to bring your father here, but alas—"

"Tek!" Cale said pointedly, cutting off the scientist's
ramblings. "Is it considered polite in Vusstran society to
leave a guest naked on your doorstep?"

Tek made a ticking sound deep in his throat and
blinked several times. "Why no, of course not. But how
often would such a situation—" Tek paused, blinked
again, cocked his head to one side, and suddenly erupted
into a hearty chuckle. "Hmm, yes. I take your point."
He scurried over to a workbench, removed a set of
cleanroom clothing, and handed it to Cale, who accepted
the garments awkwardly.

Cale shivered. "Why do you have to keep it so cold
in here, anyway?"

Tek made the ticking sound again. "I know I've
taught you something about science, my boy. Why do
you think we keep it cold in here?"

Cale had actually asked the question out of a mixture
of discomfort and embarrassment. Now, he was thrown
off balance. He ran his gaze around the high-ceilinged
rectangular room. The walls were made of the same
sturdy, ceramic-and-metal alloy that composed most of
the buildings on Vusstra, derived from recycled industrial materials.

"Well, for one thing, cooler temperatures inhibit the growth of bacteria," Cale answered. "And a cool atmosphere is also more favorable for long-term storage."

"Excellent!" Tek said, smiling with his thick lips. "Yes, you have been listening. And biological systems are altered more slowly at low temperatures, allowing us more time to do our work."

He gestured for Cale to follow him deeper into the laboratory vault. "This is primarily a storage room, and it contains some of Vusstra's most valuable resources." He walked over to a rack on one wall that held row upon row of vials, canisters, beakers, magnetic bottles, cryogenic capsules, and vacuum-sealed pods.

"Greed, waste, and pollution have caused the extinction of many Vusstran species, but all is not lost, you see." Tek's round head bobbed up and down as he read labels and then extracted one canister from a rack. He handed it to Cale.

Cale took it, squinted at the label. "*Meloplasmapod triorganus?* I, uh, hope you're not expecting me to drink this, because I pretty much lost my appetite in the decontamination booth there."

The Vusstran scientist snatched the canister back with a sound that Cale recognized as something between a snort and a laugh. Tek fumbled briefly with what appeared to be a lens on one end of the container, and a tiny holographic projection appeared in the air above it. In the image, a luminous, crimson-colored creature splashed in phantom ocean waves, parts of its body armored with what looked like pearlescent shells; with a hard, insectile leg, the creature played beautiful harplike music on its slippery, outstretched tentacles. Round, saucerlike eyes shone with a rudimentary intelligence.

Tek made a rueful clicking noise in his throat. "The last of these happy creatures died forty cycles ago, but the essence of several prime specimens—what your people would call the DNA—is contained in this." He held the canister tightly in one three-fingered hand.

"And those?" Cale's voice trailed off as he gazed at the rows of containers in the room. There must have been thousands of them, all carefully labeled, stored, and protected.

"Yes," Tek said, his voice tinged with excitement. "Each one holds a different species of plant or animal that once lived on Vusstra. They are lost to us for the moment, but someday . . ."

"Someday? Why not now? Why wait? I mean, you have the technology to bring those lost species back. You said it yourself: they're resources—your most valuable resources—right here in this room. We could bring back the *meloplasmapod triorganus* right now."

Tek shook his head. "Only to have them become lost all over again? The reasons for their extinction remain. Our water is polluted, our air is tainted. Many of the plants and microscopic organisms that made up the intricate food web no longer exist." He replaced the container in its exact spot on the long rack. "No, before we can bring back these creatures, our *planet* itself must be revived. Sam Tucker was working with me on a plan that would have helped rejuvenate a portion of Vusstra, a pilot project. Within a few more cycles, we would have finished the plan and been ready to test it."

Cale grunted. Obviously the Drej attack had brought everything to a screeching halt. "Wait, let me guess the rest. When my father escaped on the *Titan*, he had all the last pieces you needed." He looked pointedly down at his ring. "And he promised to return to help you finish your work, just like he promised to come back for me. And no one has seen him since. Does that about sum it up?"

Tek's eyes did not meet Cale's. "It was not as simple as that, Cale. Your father was a great man, a man of his word."

"Well, I wouldn't know that, would I? I don't know enough about him to tell if he kept his promises or not, except for the one I can remember. And that one he didn't keep."

"Your father and I shared a vision for a future that we could make better for our children."

"When you realized my father wasn't coming back, why didn't you just continue the work yourself?" Cale asked.

Tek spread his arms in a helpless gesture. "Some vital data was archived with the plans for the Titan Project. Unfortunately, I'm not the scientist your father was. I'm not even the scientist Ryt was. She was trying to help me reconstruct the plan, but when she died . . ." His shoulders slumped. "I'm still missing several key chemical equations."

Then he took a deep breath and straightened, finding strength and determination inside himself. "But I haven't given up hope. Someday, I'll find the archive that holds the equations, or I'll find someone else to help me. I still believe in the dream Sam Tucker and I shared. We all must have our dreams."

Cale heaved a heavy sigh. "Well, some of us don't

have much in the way of dreams." He turned toward the laboratory exit. "Right now, I'd settle for just getting out of this goofy labsuit."

As he walked through the doorway into the decontamination chamber, an electronic voice said, "Alert. Severe physical abnormalities detected."

Cale sighed again. "This time, I'd have to agree with you."

Later, Cale retreated to the workshop he and Tek had built together. In spite of the fact that Iji flitted in and out of the room, asking frequent and annoying questions, Cale could not help but feel a glow of comfort and satisfaction as he worked on one of his inventions.

Technology, at least, was one thing that Vusstra had in abundance, and Cale took advantage of it. Although he would have made scornful noises at any suggestion that he was sentimental, he still had faint, warm memories of days spent at a similar workbench with his father, tinkering on their gadgets. Now, standing at this workbench, Cale felt the same faint glow of closeness, though he would never admit it.

"What is it? Come on, tell me what it is." Iji poked her snout under Cale's arm and tried to work her head closer to the bench to see what he was making. He adjusted his microgoggles to get a better look at his work and simultaneously squeezed downward with his arm, pinching Iji's snout. She squealed and backed away.

"Go work on your own invention, Ijit," Cale snapped.

"But mine's not as interesting," she whined.

Cale blew out an exasperated breath. "If you promise to go outside for a nanocycle, I'll give you a hint."

"I will. I promise," she said. "I want to be a great inventor when I go off to group school. Just like my pod-father, and like Sam Tucker, and like you." She slipped both arms around his waist and gave him a brief hug.

Cale pretended to be irritated at her childish enthusiasm. "It floats, and it's a toy. That's all you need to know for now. If you leave me alone for a while, I'll show you how it works later."

Iji hugged him again.

"You promised to go outside," he reminded her.

She danced outside onto the balcony, then scrambled up the ladder to the rooftop platform, probably to use the astrascope since a stiff wind had blown away some of the pollution that afternoon.

"You should appreciate your pod-sister more while you have her," Tek observed mildly, surprising him. Cale hadn't heard his foster father come in.

Cale snorted. "We're together every day. What I'd really appreciate is a little peace and quiet."

"Nothing ever stays the same, Cale. Do you know how long it is until Iji celebrates her eleventh cycle?"

He did a quick mental calculation. "Only another quad-week." Then he realized the significance. "And then she'll go off to group school, to learn about Vusstran community and history and solidarity."

"Hmm, yes," Tek said. "And during these advanced studies, Vusstrans form friendships and bonds that will last a lifetime. But only by leaving their individual homes."

For some strange reason, Cale's stomach clenched. He

had never considered that such a drastic change in his lifestyle could be just around the corner.

"Did you know that Ryt and I met in group school?" Tek asked. "We were studying enviro—"

Iji burst back into the room from the direction of the balcony. "What is it? You have to tell me what it is." Her face showed splotches of discoloration that signified anxiety.

"Hey, you've only been gone a few minutes," Cale objected.

"No, not the toy," Iji said. "Come outside and see it. Something really strange." She grabbed Tek and Cale and dragged them toward the open balcony door. With a long-suffering sigh, Cale pulled the microgoggles from his eyes and followed her up the ladder onto the roof.

"Just a minute while I line it up," Iji said, looking into the astrascope, then pushed Cale's face close to the eye-piece.

He blinked, willing his eyes to refocus, expecting to see some massive gap in the cloud formations or perhaps a distant stormfront. What he saw was something that made a ball of ice form in the pit of his stomach.

The object streaking through the high atmosphere glowed a transparent blue. Something in the back of Cale's mind told him he must have seen it before, if only in a nightmare. He backed away from the astra-scope.

Tek moved forward to have a look, then gasped in surprise. "A Stinger!" He turned from the eyepiece and fixed Cale with a look of concern. "A *Drej* Stinger."

An icy wave washed over Cale, colder than the bucket of water Iji had dumped on his head the day before.

"You mean, the ones who blew up Cale's planet?" Iji asked innocently. "I thought they were gone. After they destroyed Earth, they disappeared."

"Nobody's seen any of them since before your pod hatched," Cale said. He looked to Tek for confirmation. "Right?"

Tek gave a worried nod and moved back to the astra-scope. "We had hoped that they might have retreated for good, but it seems they were merely recovering their strength."

Iji, Cale, and Tek took turns watching the Drej Stinger through the astrascope. Tek contacted the Vusstran spaceport's main control tower, which was already tracking the Stinger, but had been unable to communi-cate with it.

Then, with an eerie abruptness, the Stinger arrowed straight up out of the atmosphere and disappeared . . . as if it had discovered what it needed to know.

— 4 —

Tek needed to make one of the most agonizing decisions of his career. He'd always known this day would come.

The ominous arrival of the Drej Stinger had brought a flood of emotional concerns and conflicts that Tek thought he'd dealt with years ago. He'd feared the Drej might return someday, that they had merely been recuperating after their Mothership had destroyed Earth. He knew from searching galactic records that this had happened before.

It had happened before.

And the Drej had resurfaced stronger than ever. He had known it was possible. Yet somehow he had not been prepared.

Tek retreated to his favorite lounge-nest in the library of their home and pondered the imponderable. Unable to stay still for long, he stood and paced the floor, noiseless on his big padded feet. Had he truly been correct to raise Cale here on Vusstra, rather than in one of the tough, Human Drifter colonies? Was that what Sam Tucker would have wanted? Although Cale and Iji squabbled often, Tek could see a strong and solid bond between the two, despite the frequent altercations, practical jokes, and complaints.

But what of the boy's bond with Humans, his own kind? Had he been Vusstran, Cale would long since have entered a group school, where he would have bonded with classmates who had similar skills, interests, and ideals. Iji herself would soon have access to the support of her peers, the comfort of community, the overarching sense of belonging that Cale had yet to experience.

And now the Drej had returned. What did they want? Was it just a coincidence that they had come *here*?

Wrestling with his concerns, Tek stalked among the library volumes, too restless to settle into his lounge-nest. He felt an urgent need to leave, *soon*, but he tried to be logical. Panic would do no good. When Tek was trying to solve a problem, he often took inspiration from the biographies of important beings. Alas, no one had yet written about the life of the great Sam Tucker, though when the time was right, someone undoubtedly would. Perhaps even Tek himself.

He chose two installments from "Lives of Greatness," his favorite series. One of them was about Wens, a visionary who, two hundred cycles earlier, had recognized Vusstra's pollution problems and founded an environmental movement, just barely in time to avert the complete devastation of the world. The other was about Onluck'mur, a classical xenopsychologist who had risen to fame on Solbrecht.

One evening, with Iji and Cale curled up in lounge-nests beside him and the cermet hearth glowing a cheerful orange, Tek had tried to analyze what produced "greatness." He searched vainly for answers in his books. Facing adversity without yielding to despair seemed to be a common theme, as was the capacity to make decisions under difficult conditions and accept the consequences. Also, most heroes engaged in a struggle because it was *right*, not for personal gain.

Tek wondered if Cale Tucker had inside him the right stuff to be counted among those heroes.

Iji had certainly benefited from contact with Cale. She adored her pod-brother and often imitated his interests. Right now, while Tek pondered what to do about the Drej sighting, Cale was reading a holoscroll entitled "Mechanical Systems Analysis and Application, Part III." Meanwhile, Iji was curled up with Part I of the series.

But Iji was also surrounded by her own people. Had Cale received equivalent benefits from his association with Vusstran society? No more than a handful of Humans resided on the entire planet of Vusstra, and Cale rarely encountered one.

Upon seeing the Drej Stinger, Cale had reacted with excitement and uneasy curiosity. The boy had been so young when Earth had been destroyed—perhaps he felt no connection to those billions of Humans murdered in a single, sweeping attack.

Perhaps Tek had been mistaken to raise Cale among people who had never suffered under the Drej. Most of the time, Tek himself blocked out memories of the Earth's end, sealing the images, disappointments, and terrors of that day behind a firm barrier. The waste of it all still haunted his dreams. That beautiful planet, with so many resources intact, crumbled to space ash. For nothing! Billions of innocent people left behind because there had never been enough ships to evacuate them all. The years of research Sam Tucker and Ryt and Tek had put in during the Titan Project, much of it lost in the confusion of the evacuation.

But no, all was not lost. Tek knew deep inside that his own world could be saved. A better Vusstra could be handed down to his pod-daughter. If only he could find the data he lacked. Hadn't Sam Tucker escaped with the *Titan* itself? Other portions of the sprawling project must have been removed before the explosion. Perhaps the missing pieces of the Vusstran Renewal Plan had also been taken to safety. Tek could not give up hope. Even in the face of imminent destruction, Sam Tucker had never given up. This, as far as Tek was concerned, was one of the marks of *greatness*.

From his lounge-nest above, Cale tossed down the holoscroll he'd been reading. The coruscating letters and numbers winked out. "How useful can any of that Earth science be?" Cale wondered out loud. "It comes from a planet that let itself be destroyed by glowing blue aliens who, as far as we know, don't even use conventional machinery. I might as well just file that with all the other elementary texts, like my *Feynman Lectures on Physics*."

"Those were fun," Iji put in.

Cale rolled his eyes. "You read them when you were *four*. No Human being has made a significant contribution to science in more cycles than you've been alive.

Maybe I should be trying to get some Drej textbooks instead."

That moment decided it for Tek. He needed to continue Cale's education—about Drej, about Humans, about Earth history and culture, and about the value of solidarity. And he'd have to do it somewhere else. It was time for Cale to go to a "group school" for Humans.

Tek would just have to find one for him.

The *Ale Keg* wasn't much of a spaceship—secondhand and dented here and there—but Cale could not remember when he'd last been so excited. He and Tek and Iji spent two days making sure the *Ale Keg* was spaceworthy (as much as she needed to be, at any rate). Tek hadn't seen the need for a high-quality spaceship in years, and so had sold his, using the money to fund additional research and to purchase texts for Cale and Iji's home education. Tek had gotten the *Ale Keg* for next to nothing at a military surplus auction.

"This ship will get us as far as we need to go," he assured Cale as they worked. "Hmm, yes. We'll take it to Tau-14, a salvage station. I've got some savings and, along with whatever we get for the *Ale Keg* as a trade-in, we ought to be able to get ourselves quite a fine ship. I hear they have some Humans working on Tau-14, too. You might even have a chance to make some friends there."

Cale's mouth twisted. "What's the point in making friends with a bunch of losers? If the best job they could get was working on some salvage station, why bother?"

Tek sent Cale a stern glance. "We all have valuable

properties, and it's never wasteful to make friends. Each of us has strengths—"

"Anyway, they're Humans, like you, Cale," Iji interrupted. "Aren't you interested? I'd certainly want to make friends with them."

"*You* will be in group school by then, pod-daughter," Tek said firmly. She would be staying with Ryt's brother and his mate for the last quad-week before she joined the other selected Vusstrans in classes.

After that, Iji fell silent and spoke little. Tek tried to reason with her. "Can't we just be happy in these last few days together?"

"How can I be happy when you're deserting me?" the Vusstran girl shot back at him.

The entire exchange did not upset Cale unduly, but when the day of their departure dawned and Iji did not show up at the spaceport to see them off, Cale found himself wounded beyond anything he could have believed.

The *Ale Keg* lifted from its launchpad and soared up through the atmosphere with no sign of his little pod-sister. Cale kept his face close to the kleersteel window-port, watching, hoping that somehow at the last minute Iji would show up. "I can't believe it," he said at last, when the *Ale Keg* broke free of the atmosphere. "I knew Iji was hurt, but I thought eventually she'd come around. Doesn't she know it may be cycles before we see each other again?"

The two fell silent, each immersed in his own thoughts. Cale attempted to distract himself by going over Tek's navigational calculations. Next, he adjusted the fittings and crash restraints on all of the seats in the cockpit. Then he drew a rough schematic of the *Ale Keg*'s engines. He double-checked the fuel supply to the attitude-control thruster jets. Tek sat reading some biography or other.

As the journey continued, Cale, still restless, tightened access-panel bolts, optimized photon flow from the overhead panels, and re-stowed the emergency gear. He had just slipped back into the copilot's seat to check the navigational calculations for a third time, when he looked up and blinked. "Tek, where are we going after Tau-14? You never really told me."

"Hmm, yes. Wherever your education takes us, my boy. First, I'll try to make contact with some of your father's friends, Humans, to see if they'd like to take over the duties. If your father's friends aren't ready for it, then we'll just continue as I had planned."

Cale looked at him in surprise. "You mean, you'd just leave me in the hands of total strangers?"

"Oh, no. It's not as simple as that," Tek objected. "Besides, you're beginning to sound just like Iji."

A faint, familiar giggle wafted up from the rear of the cockpit. Cale's eyes narrowed. "No. *That* sounded just like Iji." The young man bounded up from the copilot's chair and began rummaging through cockpit cabinets. He searched unsuccessfully and muttered to himself as he looked for the source of the laughter.

He stamped his foot in frustration and was rewarded by a brief squeal from somewhere beneath him. Cale dropped to his knees and began lifting floorplates. "Hah!" Smiling in triumph, he hauled Iji out of a compartment by the scruff of her neck.

Tek dropped his bookpad and leaped to his feet. "What are you doing here?"

"I had to come," she said plaintively.

"But you're going off to group school, and—and we're not even in the Vusstran system anymore," Cale said.

"I had to come," Iji repeated, then continued all in a rush. "You didn't seem to understand how much I would miss you, and I knew you would both miss me very much, so I thought that I'm learning as much with my family as I could in any old group school, so when you said you were leaving I—"

"You had to come," Cale supplied for her.

"Exactly," Iji confirmed in a small voice.

Tek covered his eyes with the claws of his three-fingered hand. "You disobeyed me," he said, trying to sound furious, though Cale could hear from Tek's voice that he was pleased to see his pod-daughter again.

"I'm sorry, but if you let me go with you I promise not to disobey again and I'll do everything you say I promise I won't be a nuisance, I'll help with any chores that need to be done and—"

But Tek had already begun to plot their return trip to Vusstra. When he had the preliminary flight protocol calculated, he scanned the route. He muttered, shook his head, and scanned the route again.

Cale moved forward to study the control panels and gave a low whistle. "Look, another one of those Drej Stingers! Like the one we saw through our astrascope."

"Is it following us?" Iji asked.

"It's right on our flight path if we head back toward Vusstra," Cale said.

With another shake of his head, Tek erased the calculations. "Well, Iji, I guess you'll be staying with us after all."

Iji squealed with delight. Cale grinned.

Flying farther from Vusstra, they settled into a comfortable routine over the next couple of days. Several times, Tek read out loud from his biographies of great beings, considering it necessary to continue Iji's and Cale's schooling. Iji and Cale tinkered with the ship's nonessential subsystems. The better shape the *Ale Keg* was in, the more it would bring as a trade-in.

On the third day, as they were eating together, the proximity alert went off. An electronic voice said, "Two hours to salvage station Tau-14. Docking preparations will commence in one-point-five hours."

"I hope that Drej ship didn't follow us," Iji said. "They are dangerous, aren't they, Father?"

"Yes, they're dangerous," Tek said in a low voice. "The Drej have destroyed more than one planet."

"But why?" Cale wanted to know. "No one's ever been able to explain it to me."

Tek shook his large head slowly. "No one really has the answers. The Drej don't send out announcements about why they're going to attack a planet, why they target one civilization instead of another."

"It doesn't make sense," Cale said. "Earth technology wasn't nearly as advanced as the technology on Vusstra or Solbrecht or Fauldro. The Drej can't have thought we were a threat. So why pick on us?"

"Because they could?" Iji suggested. "Sometimes you pick on *me* just because I'm smaller."

Tek shook his head again. "No, there are weaker planets, even more vulnerable civilizations. The only thing we've really learned about the Drej is that when they target a culture to destroy, they want to be certain its people are defeated. They don't have to wipe out every last member of that race—just break their spirit. That's how the Drej conquer."

Cale let out a long, slow breath. "Well, looks like it's working so far. I don't see much of the Human spirit anymore."

− 5 −

On Tau-14, while Tek met with the dockmaster to negotiate trading the *Ale Keg* for a better spacecraft, Cale set out to investigate the salvage station on his own. He reveled in seeing something new for a change, a place that wasn't monotonous and dreary. At last, a place to explore that wasn't Vusstra.

The salvage station, which also served as a refueling point for travelers and traders in the area, had been built on and into an asteroid shaped like a rotten tooth. The exterior was strung with docking rings and girders and salvage bays where a motley crew of workers broke down old equipment into saleable components. Tau-14 was a place where Humans were not a rarity, where potential friends or enemies could lurk around any corner. Cale knew no one, and no one knew him, and he figured that was a good thing.

"Builds character," he assured himself.

Although Cale was in good physical condition, he was

not particularly well-muscled. Because of his youth and because Vusstrans tended to consider Humans odd-looking, regardless of how muscular they were, he'd never felt the need to build up his physique. Cale had never met any Humans he'd wanted to impress. Tek always taught him that self-confidence was all he needed. And Cale had his share of confidence—sometimes a bit more than was warranted, according to Tek.

The inside of Tau-14 was no less impressive than its outer shell. Tunnels honeycombed the rock, lined with metal plates and occasional heaters. Frequent airlock hatches led outside to space, through which work crews could easily exit to their salvage sites out in the vacuum. Also, Cale saw more different creatures on this station than he had ever seen in one place in his life. In the shipping docks alone, Cale saw Akrennians, Vusstrans, Solbrechtians, Rybets, Humans, and Mantrins, as well as other species he had only seen in padbooks or holos-crolls before.

As he wandered the passageways of the station, Cale found himself rather enjoying the dim lighting, the profusion of odors, the unusual angularity of the architecture, and the patchwork of adapted metals and machinery. Everything had been put to good use, nothing wasted. Cale didn't fool himself for a moment that all the systems were in perfect working order: Minor glitches were always to be expected when dealing with repaired, reconfigured, or recycled materials. Even so, the station was ingeniously constructed. He could probably learn quite a bit from Tau-14 about adapting parts and technology to alternate uses.

Cale usually managed to master any subject he set his

mind to—especially anything mechanical. He had a true knack that bordered on instinct. In fact, he thought, as he took a lift down to a dimly lit storage level, he could probably figure out how to run any piece of equipment on this entire salvage station. A cocky smile quirked the corner of Cale's mouth, and he pulled himself straight. He added a bit of a swagger to his walk. That would surely show anyone he happened to meet that here was *somebody*, a person to be reckoned with. Even if he was a Human.

Cale's stomach rumbled, and he followed his instincts down a maze of corridors toward a trapezoidal doorway. "Now unless I miss my guess," he murmured, "this would be"—the door shuddered and slid apart to reveal a broad room lined with dining tables and filled with smells that Cale could only describe as . . . *indescribable*—"the mess hall," he concluded with a nod of satisfaction. "And it certainly is a mess."

Before Cale had left the sealed exterior bay, the dockmaster had said, "Try our café. We've got a new cook from the Kituan sector. Most, uh, interesting cuisine you ever tasted." Vusstran food was always bland and recycled, grown in algae vats or processed from protein masses. Cale couldn't remember the last time he'd had a meal that tasted remotely "interesting."

He swaggered toward the food counter, trying not to look as if he had never done this before. Which he hadn't. Cale's mouth fell open as he gazed at the selection of dishes spread before him: noodles that wriggled, viscous sauces that moved around the plate by themselves, garnishes that looked ready to eat the main course . . . or the customer. At other tables, some burly

alien dockworkers used their fists to smash their meals
into submission before devouring them.

While Cale stared, a strange, insectoid creature suddenly appeared behind the food counter. It reminded him
of a gangly, meter-tall cockroach with spindly limbs and
long, twitching antennae perched atop its ugly head. It
wore a white chef's hat and flailed serving implements
in both arms. Cale had to press his lips together to keep
himself from laughing aloud.

"Whad'll ya have, huh?" the chef asked, chittering
rapidly. "C'mon, don't spend all day makin' a decision
here. Cantcha see I got hungry mouths ta feed? This is
good. This is good." The chef banged spoons on metal
trays with a blur of frantic motion. "This is good. This
is good."

Cale glanced around in confusion. There wasn't exactly a line forming at the food counter. "I, uh," he stam-
mered.

"Method of payment?" the cook snapped.

"C-credit?" Cale said, sounding more certain than he
felt.

The cockroach chef bounced up and down. "Right,
just passin' through then. Coulda guessed that. Which
docking bay?"

Cale scratched his blond head. "Number fifty-six, I
think. Yeah, fifty-six, upper level."

"Sure thing, kid. What'll it be then? Groonch? Flavl?
Hugga fish? Steamed brupweed? Ordl steak? Jyx pasta
surprise? Maybe a coupla nice qrind eggs? I can mix it
all together if you like. You'll have ta eat it fast
though—not responsible f'r the consequences."

Cale blinked. "Yeah, uh . . . that sounds fine."

In a flurry, the cook produced a sampler platter of what he claimed were his most famous dishes. Cale ate the entire meal alone and managed to appreciate every bite—primarily because he had no idea what he was eating. At least the growling in his stomach stopped, and his spirits were rising. He couldn't wait to continue his exploration to see what else he might find.

Well-trained by Tek, Cale took his platter, cup, and utensils to the used dish area at the end of the food counter and placed them on a moving panel that whisked them through an opening in the wall back into the kitchen, where they were bombarded by sterilization rays. Cale smiled at the cook. "Thanks. That, uh, really hit the spot."

The insectoid chef gave him a quizzical look. "Ya sure yer a Human, kid?" Then he gave a chitter of laughter and shrugged his spindly arms. "No need ta answer, but b'lieve me, I meant it as a compliment."

Cale wondered what kind of negative experiences the cockroach chef might have had with Humans, but decided to take his compliments wherever he could get them. Whistling a Vusstran marching tune, he left the mess hall and strode down the corridors, nodding at everyone he met. Some returned the greeting, others ignored him or seemed not to notice.

Nothing marred his mood—until he ran into his first Human. Literally.

Cale was just rounding a corner when he collided with a solid wall of muscle. "Hey, I'm sorry." He reeled backward to get a good look at who he had run into.

The man in front of him was probably the largest Human Cale had ever encountered. A full head taller

than Cale and half again as broad-shouldered, he flexed
his muscular arms. But he didn't speak. Another young
man, wiry and brusque, took charge, stepping in front
of Cale and pressing his face close.

"*Sorry?* Is that all you've got to say?"

The wiry man, apparently the leader, had a lean face,
olive complexion, and wavy, shoulder-length brown
hair. He wore hard-heeled black boots, tight-fitting
pants, and a flowing, rainbow-silk shirt. His storm-gray
eyes were narrowed in a look of suspicion and challenge.

"No, not at all," Cale said quickly. "I have lots more
to say. Like how great it is to see another Human being."

Just then, three more Human males stepped around
the corner to flank the first one and crossed their arms
over their chests. Each one of them seemed as massive
as the man he had run into.

"Uh, *five* Human beings," Cale corrected. "Sure, this
is great. My name's Cale." He held out a hand.

The first big man finally spoke. His voice sounded as
if he had recently swallowed rocks. "You don't really
think Klegg is going to make friends with a loser like
you, do you?"

Cale's hopeful expression faded, and he let his hand
fall to his side. "Well, why not? We're all Humans,
aren't we? I mean, Humans have to stick together,
right?"

A sneer formed on Klegg's thin-lipped mouth. "I'll
take care of this Blitz," he said to the big thug next to
him. "We stick together, when there's a good reason to."
He grinned wolfishly at Cale. "You got a good reason
for us to stick with you? Got any credits, boy? Our
friendship is for sale, see, and it doesn't come cheap."

"Not really," Cale admitted, confused at how these Humans were treating him—not at all what Tek had told him to expect. "But if you got to know me, you'd find out that I have a lot more useful qualities than just credits in an account."

Big-shouldered Blitz made a rude noise, and Cale continued in a rush, "For instance, I'm really good with machinery. I can fix just about anything, and I'm pretty creative. Tek says Humans should work together to, uh, cultivate solidarity. That's our only real hope in the universe."

Klegg's gray eyes slashed Cale with a steely glare. "I choose my own friends, and I don't need any new ones, especially little pip-squeaks like you." Cale found the description ironic, since he and Klegg were about the same size. Unless you added in the body mass of the four other bullies.

Cale sighed. It had been a long time since he'd met any new Humans, and these guys weren't making it particularly easy. Maybe the cockroach chef had good reason for his dislike of them. "I was taught that everybody has valuable qualities, and it's never wasteful to make friends. You have to find each person's strengths and . . ." He spread his arms, letting the idea sink in.

Just then, Iji appeared from behind a crate across the corridor. "Hey, you Humans should be a lot nicer to him, you know."

Cale's stomach clenched. She had been following him! This was the last thing he needed right now. "Ijit, don't," he said in a low voice, shaking his head.

She disregarded his admonition. "My father told us Humans were much kinder than this. Don't you know

who Cale is? He's the son of Earth's greatest scientist,
Sam Tucker, a famous man and a—"

Klegg gave a derisive snort. "Sam Tucker? Let's
see. . . . Wasn't he the crackpot who said he could build
a better place for Humans to live, that he would *save*
mankind? That he was the best hope for the Human
race?"

"He was a great man," Iji said.

"*Iji* . . ." Cale warned.

"And Cale is a great man, too," she added. "At least
he's going to be."

Klegg's sneer was back as he looked at Cale with new
interest. "Sam Tucker was nothing but an eccentric, ego-
maniacal crackpot." He paused for emphasis. "And
therefore, his son must be . . ."

Cale felt a simmering rage begin deep in his gut, as
if a cluster of bubbling mudpots had formed inside him.
Klegg glanced at Iji and spoke to Blitz and his burly
lieutenants. "Grab the little one. I'll take care of this . . .
fool myself."

—6—

Cale never knew who threw the first punch.

He saw red, but that might have been from somebody else's swinging fist and his own bloody nose. He hit something with his clenched hand, missed the next time, then felt his knuckles mash lips against rows of hard teeth. The grunt and splutter of pain resounded like music in his ears, until one of Klegg's tough-guy friends pounded him on the back of the head.

"Cale!" With a screech Iji dodged the thug who was trying to grab her and threw herself into the fray as well. Muscular Blitz knocked the little Vusstran girl aside as if she were made of pufferfluff.

Cale's surprise attack didn't last long. Within a few seconds, his body was bounced like an orbital ball off the curved bulkhead, and then he was on the deck in a whirlwind of kicking feet, jabbing elbows, and pounding fists.

Maybe this fight wasn't such a good idea.

Klegg's three rough companions were all shoulders and no neck. Cale couldn't tell if they wore brass knuckles or some kind of military gauntlets, but each blow that hit him felt like an asteroid impact.

As a matter of family pride and bullheaded stubbornness, Cale made a good showing, though. Pushing back to his feet, he rammed his head into Blitz's rock-hard stomach. Luckily, Cale's skull was harder than his opponent's abdomen, and the burly thug said something that sounded like "Glrrrk!" before he retched out spittle onto Cale's neck.

Cale hoped Tau-14 had shower cubicles for rent, once all this was over.

He swung his right hand up and struck underneath a second bully's chin so hard the teeth clicked audibly together. He heard a monotonous drumbeat and realized it was Klegg's fists pummeling his back and shoulder blades. The wiry ringleader managed to stay on the fringe of the fight while Cale rolled and swung and kicked against the bully's much larger companions, but Klegg darted in to do whatever damage he could, careful to keep his splendid rainbow-silk shirt unruffled.

"You leave Cale alone!" Iji sprang onto Klegg's back, gouging at the young man's eyes with her blunt, clawed fingers. When she bit down on his shirt and tore the fabric, he reacted with sudden fury.

Klegg smashed her against a metal wall, slamming her breath from her lungs. Iji fell coughing onto the deck, but her eyes were filled with anger, like a coiled werbyl ready to spring. Klegg touched the hole in his silk shirt, then stalked toward her, letting his henchmen take care of Cale.

One member of the bully quartet pinned Cale's arms behind his back while Blitz punched him smack in the eye. Then the brawny men threw him to the floor and jumped on top of him. Though it was only a small asteroid station, Tau-14 had perfectly sufficient gravity for them to accomplish this.

Klegg grabbed the scrappy Vusstran girl under the armpits and raised her off the floor. She flailed at him, all elbows and knees and feet. "Let me down!" The ringleader merely extended his arms to keep out of her reach and laughed at her helpless struggling.

On the floor, Cale spat blood from a split lip, while more trickled down from his nostrils. The thugs on top of him were as heavy as cargo containers. He tried to sit up and was shoved back down. His head hit the floor with a painful crack. He blinked, but his smashed eye was swelling shut, obscuring his vision. Tomorrow his bruised face would be as splotchy as a Vusstran's.

"We got him, Klegg," said Blitz.

Cale couldn't move.

With a sharp look on his narrow, hawklike face, the ringleader held Iji tightly around the waist and sneered at her. "I don't like it when people show disrespect toward me." Taking long strides, he walked to a heavy door on the side wall of the pressurized tunnel, one of the external emergency airlock hatches. He used his right elbow to punch the access button. "You tore my shirt, brat."

Cale saw what Klegg was doing, and his mouth went dry. He redoubled his efforts to sit up but succeeded only in raising his shoulders high enough off the cold deck that the bullies could slam him down again, hard.

The airlock door opened upward with a hiss like cold steam. The inside of the chamber was small, with rounded walls and a kleersteel observation window so that Iji could look out onto cold, airless space. Salvage operations continued all around the Tau-14 asteroid. Dismantled ships drifted like flotsam inside their docking corrals. Spacesuited crews used laser saws to cut away hull plates. Anti-grav scooters pushed big hulks off to smelting vats and vacuum stripping areas.

If Klegg ejected Iji into frozen, airless space, none of those people outside could save her. Iji understood what he meant to do. She became a wild thing, scrabbling, clawing, but the bully was much stronger. He stuffed her into the airlock chamber as if he were jamming dirty socks into a laundry scrubber-field.

Iji bounced off the thick outer hatch, hit the floor of the chamber, and sprang back to her feet. But Klegg moved too fast for her, pounding the CLOSE button so that the heavy, metal door slammed shut, sealing her inside.

"Stop it!" Cale managed to shout, his words slurred by pain. He spat blood onto the metal deck, adding another stain to the many already there.

Klegg stood next to the controls, tapping his fingers beside the buttons. He looked down at his torn shirt, scowled, and turned back to the airlock.

Cale raised his head enough to see that with a single code, the wiry bully could cycle out all the air from the emergency chamber. He could open the outer door and eject Iji to a cold, suffocating death in open space.

Klegg smiled. Then he laughed.

Cale fought harder, and the ringleader finally said,

"Let him sit up. It'll be better if he gets to see her. One last time."

"Aww, I'm getting all misty-eyed," one of the bullies said.

Behind the kleersteel of the sealed airlock, Iji pounded with her flat hands, searching for some kind of emergency override inside the chamber, but she found none. Her terrified face pressed against the window, looking out with pleading eyes and genuine fear. She stared at Cale, ignoring the thick-necked bullies, as if fully confident that her pod-brother would rescue her. Somehow.

Cale didn't know what to do.

"I can see how she must be an annoying little kid, Cale," Klegg said. "In fact, I'll probably be doing you a favor by shooting her out into space. You wouldn't miss an ugly alien brat like that, would you?"

Cale spat more blood out and "accidentally" targeted Blitz. "Let her out of there. This is getting out of hand." He couldn't believe these young men would actually commit murder. But he also knew that some Humans didn't see killing an alien as anything too terrible.

"Out of hand?" Klegg said, then plucked at his torn shirt again. "It hasn't *begun* to get out of hand yet."

Iji stopped pounding and just stared at Cale. "I'm sure she didn't mean any disrespect," he said.

"But you did," Blitz replied and cuffed him on the ear.

Cale shook his head to clear his vision. He tried to open his swollen eye and glared at Klegg, ignoring the other thugs. Those four weren't important. "Let her out." Then through clenched teeth, he bit out the last word, "*Please.*"

Klegg circled his finger in a taunting caress around the airlock controls. "I'm not unreasonable," the ring-leader said. "If you've got anything of value, maybe you can buy back the brat's life. Seems to me, I own it right now."

That brought Cale up short. He didn't have anything left, and he certainly owned no trinkets of value. His pockets were empty. What could these bullies possibly want? "But I don't—"

Blitz cuffed him on the side of the head again. "If your father's some great Human scientist, don't tell me you have no credits."

"But I don't. That was a long time ago—"

Klegg let his finger hover in front of the airlock button. "Oh, well. Sorry we couldn't do business with you, Cale Tucker." Iji pounded frantically on the kleersteel windowport, her thumps muffled behind the thick hatch.

Klegg made as if to jab forward, but Cale surged up to his knees, fighting against the thugs who held him. "Wait!" He looked at the bully to his left, saw a cut on his grease-smudged cheek where his ring had broken the man's skin.

"I've got a ring. It was my father's, a real artifact of Earth." He held up his left hand so that Klegg could see the gold band on his middle finger. "Fine workmanship. I'm sure it's worth a lot."

Klegg moved his finger away from the airlock button. "Let me see it."

Cale shook off the viselike grip on one arm though a second bully maintained his hold on the other. Did they think he would break away and run? With Iji trapped in the airlock?

Cale looked down at the ring, remembered how Sam Tucker had given it to him at their moment of parting. *I want you to always keep this with you.* Cale told himself it didn't mean all that much, just a sentimental trinket, a reminder of memories he wished he didn't have. Not long ago, he'd tried to throw it away in the bubbling mudpots. Now maybe the ring could do some good. It could save Iji's life.

He yanked the ring off his finger. Klegg snatched it, scrutinizing it under the garish tunnel light. "It's ugly," he said. Then he frowned at Cale. "But who knows? Maybe I can melt it down, make a nice new tooth to wear."

Cale wanted to remove a few of the ringleader's teeth himself, but he held his tongue.

Klegg flipped the ring in the air like a coin and caught it in the palm of his hand. He looked down appraisingly, and smirked. "Why not? I'll be generous today. We've got to get back to New Marrakech anyway."

He stepped away from the airlock controls and motioned for the last bully to release Cale. "Come on, we've wasted enough time. I'm sure our cargo's loaded by now. Let's head back to the Drifter colony. I can't stand this dirt hole a minute longer." Laughing like a group of primates lower on the evolutionary scale than Humans, they swaggered away down the corridor.

Cale lunged to his feet, ignoring the ache in his muscles and bones. He wiped blood from under his nose, then lost his balance as his left leg buckled beneath him. He looked down the empty, sloping tunnel, but Klegg and his companions were already gone.

More carefully this time, Cale climbed back to his

feet, staggered to the airlock door, and punched the release button. When the door slid upward with a hiss, Iji spilled out. She gasped as if all the air had already been drained from the small chamber. "Do you think they would have really shot me out into space?" she asked, her eyes huge.

Cale wasn't convinced, but it was not a risk he'd been willing to take. "I don't know. Sometimes bullies just like to show off."

"That's easy when there's five of them against two of us," Iji said. She grabbed his hand with her clawed fingers and made cooing, disappointed noises. "They took your father's ring. You gave them your *ring* to save me."

"It's not important." He shrugged and then winced at the pain. "No big deal. That ring didn't mean that much to me."

Iji put her hands on her hips in a defiant gesture. "Don't you lie to me, Cale Tucker."

He hesitated a moment. "I'm not lying when I say that what I'd value most right now is a hot shower and a change of clothes. One of those creeps drooled all over me." He wiped the back of his neck, frowning in disgust. "Come on, Ijit, let's get back to Tek and see if he's found a new ship yet. We've got more important things to worry about."

— 7 —

Tek was so delighted at having acquired a classic TR-Epsilon Z spaceship that he hardly noticed Cale's roughed-up condition. In all fairness, Cale supposed bruises and a black eye were insignificant skin discolorations compared to the normal splotchiness of Vusstrans. If anything, Tek probably thought Cale looked healthier than usual.

"Hmm, yes. I didn't hear back from any of your father's friends, so we're clear to push on with our travel plans," was all Tek said.

Still stinging from the encounter with Klegg and his thugs, Cale didn't go out of his way to explain what had happened, nor did he point out the loss of his father's ring. For now, the blinding physical pain swept all other thoughts from his mind. "This is not a problem," he muttered under his breath. "I can fix this." He quickly patched himself up, took a broad-spectrum, multispecies analgesic, and set to work checking out their new vessel.

The TR-Epsilon Z was a venerable craft, outdated enough to be considered a collector's model by aficionados who preferred to talk about the "golden days" rather than get new ships. The ship had been lovingly maintained and reconditioned so that it flew fast and handled well. But it looked old-fashioned. Still, it was better than their former wreck, the *Ale Keg*.

Tek flew the new ship away from Tau-14, leaving the salvage and refueling station behind. He was content in his rounded pilot's seat, running his clawed fingers over the controls like a miser sifting through his jewels.

Cale fidgeted in the seat beside him, trying to find a comfortable position. The bent back of the chair pressed at odd places against his spine; the armrests seemed uneven and his bruises already ached again. Obviously, the chair had not been designed for Human anatomy (not that many things were, especially since the Drej attack). Humans were far down on the list of preferred customers in galactic merchandising groups.

When the TR-Epsilon Z got up to speed, the artificial gravity disengaged briefly while the drive switched over to cruising mode, and Cale's straw-colored hair floated up away from his eyes, then drifted back down into his field of vision. He would have to give himself a haircut, he supposed. Absentminded Tek never noticed when the young Human needed grooming, and Cale certainly didn't trust Iji to give him a trim. His pod-sister would probably shave his head and call it attractive.

Iji was overwhelmed that Cale had sacrificed his father's ring to rescue her. Though she felt sad for his loss,

Iji kept his secret from Tek. Best of all, she proved to be less pesky for at least a while. But in the confined space of their new vessel, he supposed it wouldn't last much longer.

"So where exactly are we going next?" Cale asked, releasing a heavy sigh through his cracked lips. "And why are we going there?"

Tek looked over at him, a sorrowful expression on his jowly alien face. He puffed out his cheeks. Growing up on Vusstra, Cale had learned to read the alien's expressions.

"No one knows why the Drej targeted Earth for destruction a decade ago," Tek said. "Thirty years before that, the Drej annihilated another species, the Qu'utians." His shoulders bobbed in a rolling shrug. "I am hoping to learn why."

"It would be nice if the Drej gave people fair warning," Cale said. "I mean, so we could maybe say 'excuse me' for whatever we did that offended them so much."

He remembered the frantic, last-minute preparations on Earth as refugees scrambled aboard every possible spacecraft, anything to take them off planet in time. Cale had been only five, had understood little of the impending disaster. Many of the ragtag craft, not rated for safety, had blown up during flight; others had been destroyed by molten planetary debris. No one knew exactly how many of Earth's billions had survived. The refugees, now scattered throughout the Spiral Arm, had formed hodgepodge Drifter colonies in unclaimed space or worked as cheap laborers in industrial facilities. The Human race had no home, no place to gather, and so they just wandered.

The fact that the Drej had destroyed another planet, another race, was news to him. "Nobody knows why they went after the Qu'utians either?"

Tek shook his head. "Hmm, no. That's why we're going to the Qu'ut system."

"And what are we going to find there?" Cale asked.

Tek punched the acceleration buttons and their ship leaped into high-velocity flight with a satisfying roar from the old-style, reconditioned engines. "Answers, I hope. We won't know until we get there."

The asteroid field was like a bombing range in space.

Cale sat in the copilot's seat, his good eye as narrowed with fear as his black eye was from swelling. Tek, though, seemed to be enjoying himself. He dodged the rolling mountains that filled the black vacuum ahead, a rubble field that stretched out across half a planetary orbit.

"*That* used to be a planet?" Iji asked, poking her head between the two cockpit chairs.

"Yes, Qu'ut Prime," Tek said. Rocks, pebbles, and dust made a constant hissing, crackling sound as they vaporized against the protective shields. "Just a world's worth of debris now." Then a large meteoroid bounced off of their front shields, making the ship rock and sway.

Through clenched teeth Cale said, "How about we just concentrate on flying, huh?"

The Vusstran scientist looked over his shoulder. "Better get back to your seat, Iji, and strap in. I don't want you hurt."

"Look out!" Cale shouted as a giant, rotating rock curved toward them and crossed their path.

Tek yanked back on the ether-rudders and applied a blast from the attitude control jets. The TR-Epsilon Z swung sideways, throwing Cale against the seat. He had the delightful sensation of rediscovering every one of his bruises, welts, and wounds. As he looked out the side window, Cale saw pocked craters and the remnants of crushed mountain ranges scrape by the kleersteel port. Tiny meteorites splattered against the ship's defensive screens.

"What are we supposed to find here in this mess, Tek?" Cale said. "You want me to glean some insights into the fate of humanity from the shapes of these asteroids? I don't see much left of this Qu'utian planet except a junkyard of rocks."

"Hmm, no. This is what remains of Qu'ut Prime." The smooth skin above Tek's lantern eyes furrowed. "But that's not what we came to see. We are going to investigate Qu'ut *Minor*."

"Oh. Good." Cale rolled his eyes, bringing a fresh stab of pain in the swollen one. "I'm sure that'll be a lot more fascinating."

"Qu'ut Minor is still in one piece—mostly—and this is the only way I know of getting there," Tek explained.

Their ship continued to zigzag through the asteroid field, skipping around huge obstacles, crashing through small ones. The ring of planetary debris in the Qu'utian solar system had created a good security fence. Navigation was quite hazardous, and no enemies could easily penetrate to prey upon survivors, if there were any.

Of course, Cale realized, the asteroid field would also discourage supply ships or rescue workers. Qu'ut Minor was isolated, and any survivors would have had to fend for themselves in the four decades since the Drej had targeted their civilization.

Hours later, Cale heaved a heartfelt sigh of relief when they finally emerged on the inner boundary of the swath of rubble. Their new ship had suffered only a few scrapes and bangs, no major hull damage, no breaches, no sudden decompressions. Just the way he liked it.

Unfortunately, they still had to make their way back *out*.

"Hmm, yes. We can see Qu'ut Minor now." Tek called up an image locator on the cockpit window grid.

Ahead, a bright dot grew into a ball, lit by fiery light from the system's deep-orange sun. From afar, the lone planet looked like an open wound that had not healed even after four decades.

Iji stared out the kleersteel ports, looking for any sign of surviving civilization. Cale attempted to decipher the comm system. "Should I try to raise anyone on the hailing frequencies? They probably don't get many visitors."

Tek looked sadly at him. "Hmm. I'm afraid there's no one there to respond, Cale. Their civilization was destroyed. If there *are* any Qu'utian survivors, I doubt they'd be listening for transmissions."

He gestured at the sparkling banner of asteroids they had just passed through. "When the Drej destroyed Qu'ut Prime, the exploding debris was hurled out with such great force that major chunks intersected the orbit of Qu'ut Minor, its companion planet. The rubble bombarded Qu'ut Minor, leveling cities, starting wildfires. The climate was altered, and the atmosphere became practically unbreathable. I suspect that most Qu'utians who survived the initial attack died within months from starvation and fires."

Tek frowned again. "On Vusstra, we poisoned our planet slowly so that we learned to adapt, and we pretended not to see the damage we were doing."

As he brought the TR-Epsilon Z into low orbit, Tek surveyed the scarred world, searching for cities, power sources, life-forms. "Hmm, yes. It seems there are still a few settlements. So the Drej didn't obliterate the Qu'utians entirely, though their civilization may be unrecognizable by now."

"Aren't we going to go down and see?" Iji unstrapped again and came forward. "We've come this far."

"Sit down, Ijit," Cale said. Iji ignored him.

"Yes, we'll take the ship down." Tek began their descent, heading through the atmospheric turbulence toward blackened, geometrical masses that marked out the boundaries of once-great cities. "Think about this as we go to explore, Cale." Tek's voice was filled with a teacher's intensity. "The Drej did the same thing to your world, to your species. And now the Drej are reawakening. We've already seen their scout ships on Vusstra."

Cale swallowed hard. "So who's next? Will the Drej come after Humans again, or will they find someone else they don't like?"

Tek nodded somberly. "That is a question the entire Spiral Arm would like to have answered."

At the height of Qu'utian civilization, its cities must have been stunning examples of ethereal architecture, breathtaking in their innovative use of resources.

"This place is a dump," Cale said.

As they stepped away from the landed ship, Cale, Tek, and Iji looked around at collapsed buildings and blackened monuments, damaged long ago by raging fires. Some of the tallest buildings looked as if they had been knocked to their knees, sucker punched into submission.

They walked together down what had been a broad boulevard. Sprawled across their way lay a broken statue four stories high, a mammoth sculpture of a delicate, proud-looking creature with an elongated, narrow face, a flattened nose, and long, furlike growths in patches on its skin.

The statue seemed to have been shattered by an impact shock wave that knocked it sideways. The ancient, stoic face was chipped and pitted from flying debris. Cale looked around the empty, silent streets as the orange light of sunset cast a glow like embers dying in the sky. Even on low buildings that had survived the worst ravages of the asteroid impacts, Cale could not find a single window intact. The air smelled sour, heavy with death, even after so many decades.

"Our scanners picked up life-forms," Tek said. "Not millions, but a few survivors. They must be attempting to pick up the pieces of their civilization."

Cale scrutinized the growing shadows, but saw no movement. "Maybe they're afraid we're selling something."

"I hope they're not cannibals," Iji said. As soon as the words were out of her mouth, reverberating drumbeats like an amplified heartbeat sounded from the supposedly empty buildings. A fast, slapping, tom-tom cadence was answered by a lower tympanic beat farther down the boulevard. Then, behind them, the brassy, regal sound of a gong shattered the hushed atmosphere.

Dark-feathered scavenger birds rose from roosts in the tangled girders of decapitated skyscrapers. They made a raucous, ear-grating sound, but Cale paid little attention to them. "Uh, did we bring any weapons along, Tek?" he asked.

Tek shrugged. "Hmm, no. We're just a survey team on a research expedition. I didn't intend to do any hunting."

"Never hurts to be prepared." Cale drew a quick, cold breath.

He saw shadowy forms moving behind the broken eye sockets of windows. Something dashed across a narrow alley to his left, low to the ground, like a salamander with fast-moving arms and legs. The inky shadow was gone before he could whirl and see it clearly.

"Something's moving over there." Iji pointed frantically in a different direction.

The drumbeats grew louder, more and more joining the tempo. Now the pounding rhythms were accompanied by high-pitched whistling, like some kind of a musical code.

Cale grabbed his foster father's arm. "You think maybe we should all get back to the ship?" Iji trotted out ahead of them, but before they could get far, humanoid shapes appeared, but long and gaunt, running close to the ground like lizards scuttling over hot rocks. The newcomers cut them off from their retreat.

Cale looked back at the giant, fallen statue; more forms were climbing over it with long, spotted arms and claw hands. Their skin was smooth and moist-looking, covered with patches of colored moss, like downy feathers. The creatures moved with a liquid grace, whistling and hooting. They climbed over the fallen monument and dropped down to the uneven flagstones on the boulevard.

"Are those . . . the Qu'utians?" Cale asked.

"What's left of them, I believe," Tek answered. Cale detected a nervous quaver in Tek's voice. "Their race used to be proud and regal, a grand civilization of dreamers and artisans. Qu'utian imagination and creativity was renowned throughout the Spiral Arm."

The gaunt aliens came closer, still singing their strange music. Cale, Iji, and Tek stood back to back, though they were outnumbered by a hundred to one.

"I suppose it'd be too much to hope that you just happen to speak their language," Cale said.

"We speak," the nearest Qu'utian said, stopping in front of them as the other ethereal creatures surrounded them, drawing the ring tighter. Curious, or threatening. "We understand."

The Qu'utians raised their arms with a flurry, darting about. Their repeated words echoed in a breathy whisper. "We remember."

"We remember, too," Tek said. "My companions and I came through the asteroid field to find out what was left of the great Qu'utian civilization."

Cale took a deep breath and looked at the tall, thin aliens drawing closer. Too close. He felt closed in. To be honest, he hadn't had a very good couple of days since they had left Vusstra . . . and he wasn't that crazy about Tek's desolate, industrialized planet, either.

"Look," Cale said, "the Drej destroyed my planet and my race, just like they did yours. We just came to learn—to learn what we could about why it happened."

At the mention of the Drej, the Qu'utians began to whistle and hoot to each other. "Drej!" the leader said, drawing himself up so that he looked even more like a giant, upright salamander. His fiery eyes grew brighter.

"I'm a Human," Cale said. "I'm from Earth, and the Drej destroyed Earth." He gestured at the sky where the sparkling scarf of the asteroid field gleamed in the orange-red light of the nearby sun. "Earth is like that now. Like your Qu'ut Prime. My people are scattered across the Spiral Arm, since we have no home anymore." He was surprised at his own words, at the pride and hurt he heard in his voice.

The mossy, slippery-skinned Qu'utians pressed closer, intrigued now. Cale had their full attention. "Come with us," the leader said.

Cale, Tek, and Iji had no choice but to follow. The Qu'utians moved with long strides on spindly legs, flitting from hiding place to hiding place. Their movements had a dreamlike grace that made Cale feel clumsy.

The aliens hurried them down the broken boulevard. Iji stumbled on an uprooted cobblestone, but Tek caught his pod-daughter's arm and steadied her as they were whisked along.

A yawning door in a devastated building hung open in front of them, leading into a cavelike chamber strewn with fallen bricks and hardy weeds that had clawed their way up through cracks in the desolate architecture.

"Inside." The leader gestured with a long, smooth arm.

Cale balked, but the gathered Qu'utians pushed them forward into the dimness. He was afraid the damaged building might topple around them. What if the roof collapsed or the walls tumbled in? But the intent aliens did not pause. Perhaps with their glittering eyes, they could see in the dark better than Cale could.

"Are we being taken prisoner?" Cale could make out the dim outlines of a small room. He found walls around him and a narrow opening. Tek stumbled, and Iji ran into him.

The Qu'utian leader didn't answer, but other damp-skinned aliens pushed the travelers through the opening into a tiny closet, barely large enough for the three of them to fit inside.

"Wait! Tell us what you want," Cale said. He clenched his fists, ready to come out swinging, but remembered how easily Klegg and his bullies had defeated him the last time he'd fought back. He certainly couldn't fight an entire city full of angry Qu'utians.

"Okay, now what?" Cale said as Tek and Iji bumped into each other in the tiny chamber.

Suddenly, the floor dropped out from beneath them.

— 8 —

Of the three, Iji yelled the loudest as they fell—
though Cale and Tek both added their voices with
respectable volume. The tiny holding chamber plunged,
rocketing downward below the ruined Qu'utian metropolis.

When he stopped yelling to take a deep breath, Cale
felt the hum of motors and realized that they were falling
in a powered descent. "It's an elevator!" he shouted.

They dropped so fast that Cale's hair lifted in the air,
and he floated, as if in zero-gravity aboard a spaceship.
Iji clung first to Cale's arm, then to Tek's shoulders.

"Hmm, yes. The Qu'utians are sending us somewhere," Tek said. "On purpose."

"Well, it wasn't anything *I* said to them," Cale responded quickly. "At least I don't think so." His cheeks
flapped as the gravitational force yanked at him whenever he opened his mouth. "Maybe I shouldn't have
mentioned being a Human." He'd hoped the decimated

aliens would have felt some sort of camaraderie with another of the Drej's victims. "Silly me."

Then, with a whining, grinding sound, their descent slowed. The elevator chamber creaked, and Cale's stomach dropped back out of his throat. He felt gravity again just in time for Tek and Iji to tumble in a heap on top of him. Iji's heel thumped into Cale's swollen black eye. "Oww!"

Before the three of them could pick themselves up and try to look presentable, the chamber door slid open—revealing a subterranean wonderland.

Iji scrambled out, stepping on Tek's back and Cale's shoulder as she pushed herself away from the descent chamber. They emerged into a misty grotto, absorbing the images as quickly as their eyes could look up and around. The marvelous, underground civilization was filled with magnificent, soaring buildings, interconnected walkways, and lacy arches that looped across the vast cavern ceiling. The cave was so immense that Cale thought the Qu'utians must have hollowed out half of their world.

Iji's already large eyes became wide and round, as a flapping kite puttered along a hundred feet over her head, pedaled by a Qu'utian whose long legs pumped furiously to keep the propellers moving. Guided balloons added splashes of color across the artificial sky. Two widely spaced surrogate suns blazed at opposite ends of the grotto. Cale could barely see the other side, lost in the damp mist where the roof crust met the floor.

On the uneven rock ceiling, in shadowed spots between the blazing miniature suns, glowing, moving trails of algae made brilliant spangles that imitated constellations—perhaps so the underground Qu'utians could still remember what their sky had looked like.

A tall Qu'utian stepped in front of them, startling Cale. He guessed from the Qu'utian's slightly softer features that she might be female. Her moist, slippery skin was covered with long, mossy patches of silver-green, possibly a sign of great age.

"It is too late to ask for your promise to keep our secret." The alien's musical voice sounded like a struck crystal. "But it is not too late to prevent you from leaving, should we decide you are a threat. We have taken the liberty of moving your ship to an enclosed area in the city ruins—for your own protection, as well as ours."

"We are *not* a threat," Iji said, indignant.

Tek put a firm hand on his pod-daughter's shoulder and nudged Cale and Iji forward. The elevator door whisked shut again, and the capsule was sucked straight upward like a bullet. "My name is Tek, and this is my pod-daughter, Iji."

The tall Qu'utian female bent low, narrowing her large purple eyes.

"This Human is Cale Tucker," Tek continued. "His world was also destroyed by the Drej." Cale tried to rake his blond hair back into place with one hand, self-conscious of how messy he must look. But, judging by the hairy, mosslike growths on the tall Qu'utian's body, he didn't have to worry about *his* grooming.

The tall alien twitched her angular arms, moving with a flowing grace as if she had cartilage instead of solid bones. Her nostrils flared on her long, smooth-skinned face, and she stepped back. "Ahhh, the Drej have chosen another target." She stepped back again and made a sweeping gesture with her claw-fingered hands. "Since you are here, Human, I see that the Drej have not succeeded in defeating your race, either."

Cale couldn't tell if her facial features formed a smile, or a frown. "Well, there's not much left of my civilization, if that's what you mean," he said. "A few scattered, dirty, Drifter colonies, some teams of migrant laborers assigned to hazardous jobs. Not exactly what I'd call the Golden Age of mankind."

The Qu'utian pressed her face so close he could smell the clammy dampness of her breath. Her violet eyes blazed. "Perhaps you just don't see it." She stretched out her slippery arms again to indicate the immense grotto. "Sometimes it is preferable to hide the best that your race has to offer, rather than lose it again."

Cale didn't know what she meant.

The alien stepped away from the closed elevator shaft with a bouncing gait. "I am called Nikla, the shaman of my people. I sing to the memories of the stars. I listen to the breaths of our sleeping world. The Qu'utians dream of a new civilization, and someday our dreams will come true."

The Qu'utians' underground buildings were tall, thin tubes, like the pipes of an ancient organ, studded with holes for windows. The ethereal aliens swung from one tube to another, or walked across thin bridges, dancing, using their long arms for balance. Fountains and mist-jets sprayed water vapor into the air to keep the aliens' skin moist.

Multicolored bubbles drifted about like a swarm of balloons, and each time the spheres struck one another, a beautiful tinkling tone rang out, filling the air beneath Qu'ut Minor with music.

"This is what we have built since the Drej destroyed Qu'ut Prime." A note of pride resonated in Nikla's voice.

Cale spluttered in astonishment. "But that—that's only been decades. How could you do so much in—"

"We worked," the shaman said. "We worked *hard*. Our survivors united to preserve what they could, to protect what they remember, so our offspring do not forget. While memory lives, a civilization does not die."

Her silvery-green growths flickered as if her skin had come alive, agitated by her emotions. "The Drej may have hurt us, but they did not destroy us. We were wounded, but not defeated." Nikla leaned forward, her entire focus on Cale. "And the Drej must continue to *believe* they have won, until we become stronger than they are."

"Stronger than the Drej?" Iji said. "How are you going to do that?"

"By *succeeding*." Nikla's voice was utterly without doubt or reservations.

The shaman led them to where a waterfall seeped through a crack in the strata high above. A cool, pure shower drifted down in a silvery stream that fanned out into mist as it reached the bottom of the grotto. Pipes extended from the freshwater pool in a webwork toward the flutelike buildings that stretched to the ceiling. Emerald-green algae spread like a lawn around the waterfall basin. Squat reptilian animals grazed on the thick growths, slurping loudly.

Another putterkite swooped overhead, this one scarlet,

blue, and yellow. The kite pilot carried sacks with small parachutes, which he tossed into the open windows of the cylindrical dwelling complexes or dropped down to groups of picnickers. Cale thought it must be some sort of postal service.

"This world underground is our rebirth," Nikla said. "The Qu'utians have sculpted a new civilization from the ashes of the Drej holocaust." She craned her long neck in a sweeping arc. "It is the best of our civilization, reborn from destruction." Then she swept her arms together and glared at Tek, Iji, and Cale. "But it is hidden from the Drej. We must keep it a secret. The Drej must think we are utterly defeated—*or they will come again.*"

The shaman took them to the nearest wall, where wide, overlapping shelves of fungus grew out of the rock like broad, ivory-colored awnings. Cale sneezed as they passed beneath the frilly gills, releasing a shower of fine spores. The shaman didn't seem to notice. She bent her long body low to duck under the cluster of shelf mushrooms, and Cale noticed a concealed door, barely tall enough for Iji to walk through; the shaman had to crawl.

They found themselves within another set of rounded grottoes, pockets left by gas bubbles in cooling lava during the formation of the planet. Algae drooped like seaweed from the chamber walls, dotted with fleshy orange flowers that looked like tiny meteors trapped among the rubbery leaves. Tunnels extended farther inward, opening into other chambers.

The air was thick and steamy, like living inside a hot cloud. Nikla drew a deep breath as the moisture settled on her skin. "Some Qu'utians prefer to live here, inside the rock with heavy walls all around them, while others, who remember the sky best, choose the cylindrical tubes for their homes."

"What about the survivors we saw up on the surface?" Tek said. "The buildings seemed ruined, everything falling apart, yet still we found many of your people. Why didn't you make some repair efforts up in some of your magnificent cities?"

The shaman whirled, ducking to miss a low-hanging portion of the dimpled ceiling. "Because the Drej would *see*. Volunteers stay in the ruined cities to maintain the image of defeat. Our race must appear utterly beaten. We must appear not to be a threat."

"I don't envy the ones who get that assignment," Cale said. "What did they do, lose the lottery?"

"They serve," Nikla said. "We all serve."

Tek explored the cave, inspecting the amenities enjoyed by the underground survivors. "You did all this when the Drej were recuperating, didn't you?"

"Yes." The shaman bobbed her head again, her gray-green tendrils flopping about like a feather dance. "The Drej are made of energy. When they destroy a world, the power drain is enormous, and they must go dormant for years.

"While the Drej were recharging, our survivors were very busy. We trained our best pilots. We excavated minerals from the asteroid field—the rubble that remained of Qu'ut Prime, the heart of our civilization." Her long face grew somber. "We brought in resources. We sold every trinket we could salvage in order to purchase what we could not find ourselves. Luckily, we Qu'utians still had our knowledge, and we still had our drive."

Her violet eyes blazed with the intensity of her dream. "We manufactured the commodities we needed. We set up new ecosystems here within the grotto. We stockpiled supplies and kept our secret. See what we have accomplished?"

Cale realized that, despite his instinctive scorn for hopeless dreams, he was impressed by these Qu'utians. He couldn't believe that any Human—not even the supposedly great Sam Tucker, whose overblown dreams had wasted his precious time—could have achieved something so wonderful.

But though Tek had always told him he should spend more time with his people and appreciate the legacy of his own race, Cale doubted that Human survivors were building such a wondrous place on a hollow moon. He just didn't believe they had it in their hearts.

"Threats come in different disguises," the Qu'utian said. "We have begun to research the Drej. Little is known about their race, their technology, or the way they think. Why did they consider us a danger to them—so much that they felt the need to conquer us?

Nikla shrugged her bony shoulders and turned to Cale again. "Why did they consider *you* a danger? Why did Humans frighten them enough that they would use most of their energy to destroy your planet, forcing themselves to go dormant for years? We intend to find the answers. We will develop a way, someday, to stop their evil. The Qu'utians are a strong and determined race. We will find a way to repay the Drej for what they did to us. And to stop them. Permanently. Do not doubt it."

"That'll be a good enough revenge," Cale said.

But the stern shaman drew herself tall, rising to the ceiling of the small chamber. "No, not for revenge. We plan to make sure that this will never happen again to any race—like yours, or mine."

− 9 −

Cale had not set out to admire the Qu'utians. Before coming to Qu'ut Minor, he would have been willing to bet that no "loser" race would ever earn his esteem. But he had been wrong.

With each new accomplishment and piece of technology Cale saw, his respect for them grew. Tek seemed to alternate between amazement and curiosity, asking question after question of their shaman guide. Iji bounced along beside them, interjecting her own questions, and occasionally stopping to grab Cale's arm and point out a vertical garden, a new form of transportation, an aquafarm, or jewel-winged bats.

Faced with the ingenuity and perseverance of the Qu'utians, Cale was forced to reassess his judgment. By all rights, these people should have been humbled, defeated, hopeless. Yet Cale saw none of that. On the contrary, the Qu'utians exhibited determination, purpose, even happiness.

Tek was in deep conversation with the shaman. "Hmm, yes. In a manner of speaking, you've reclaimed more of your planet than my people have." He sighed and rubbed his hands thoughtfully together. "But we have no outside enemy to blame. We Vusstrans caused the damage to our own environment."

Nikla gave a trill of empathy. "Then your task is difficult indeed."

As he looked up at the wall beside them, Cale noticed a symbol as large around as he was tall. It consisted of a circle made from some sort of cable or wire studded with stylized thorns; a strong, simple sword plunged through the center of the ring. He realized he had seen the symbol several times since coming underground: over doorways, on clothing, stenciled onto kites or balloons. Then, to Cale's surprise, he realized that Nikla also had the same design tattooed on her shoulder, half-hidden by her tendrils of lichen-fur.

"Excuse me," Cale broke in. "What does that design with the circle and sword mean? It looks . . . impressive."

The shaman's mossy tendrils ruffled and fluttered. "The symbol is very important to us. The outer circle represents a spikevine. In ages past, the majority of Qu'utians were farmers. Those who worked hard flourished and became wealthy; others who did not plan ahead became marauders and stole from those who had enough.

"Rather than allow themselves to be beaten down, the farmlords planted spikevine, surrounding their holdings with impenetrable hedges, leaving only small openings that were easy to defend. In this way, the farmlords could still work in peace and provide for their people. Over the centuries, spikevine came to represent both prosperity and peaceful self-defense. In a more abstract sense, it also signifies victory through inner strength." She bowed her head. "We have often considered it ironic that when the Drej destroyed Qu'ut Prime, the rubble formed a spikevine fence in space."

"And the sword?" Cale prompted.

The old shaman nodded. "The sword, too, has many meanings. On the simplest level, the sword is a weapon, representing willingness to fight if one must. But that particular sword was the emblem of a great leader on Qu'ut Prime. During a dark time in our history, thousands of cruel feudal lords sprang up. Many held slaves. Many expanded their territories by killing their neighbors and annexing their lands.

"During this dark time, one lord rose up who was different from the rest, Alanth the Great. He said that blades should be used only as tools to shape our world. A sword, he said, should never be raised against a neighbor to take what is rightfully theirs. His people swore allegiance to his blade and defended themselves only when necessary.

"Alanth's kingdom grew more prosperous, and each year he offered an alliance with one or two of his neighbors. Those who accepted swore allegiance on the sword. In return, they received a pledge of safe, fair trading, and the promise of protection should they ever be attacked. Other feudal lords banded together and attempted to overthrow Alanth, but all of these campaigns were short-lived and contributed to the downfall of the lords who had begun them.

"After one hundred twelve years of ruling, Alanth had brought every kingdom under a central rule. Never once in all the years of his rule did Alanth set out to attack another kingdom to add it to his alliance. Each one joined of its own free will. Therefore, his sword symbolizes both unity and persistence. Since his time, our government has been based on his model."

Nikla looked up at the tall symbol carved on the stone wall, touched the tattoo on her shoulder. "After the Drej came, the Qu'utian survivors formed a new government, still in the model of Alanth. Our first shaman in the aftermath chose this symbol to go with the motto of 'Victory Through Persistence.' The design itself we call the Qu'utchaa."

Day never actually dawned beneath the surface of Qu'ut Minor, so Cale had no way of judging how much time had passed since they'd arrived. They rested inside guest chambers within one of the tall, cylindrical buildings.

Cale's head spun from all the information he was trying to absorb. He had not actually slept more than three hours, but instead had lain awake thinking of the things that he had seen and learned that day, still marveling at Qu'utian ingenuity.

The more he thought about it, the more he wished he could be like these Qu'utians. But Cale had to admit that he frequently let negative thoughts get the better of him. Too often, he gave in to anger, defeat, or despair, turning his own disappointment into criticisms of Vusstra, or Iji, or Humans in general, and his father in particular.

"Gotta work on that," he murmured, tossing and turning on the gelatinous mattress. The Qu'utians put great stock in their symbol. Their Qu'utchaa helped them identify with their past and remember what they had accomplished. It represented hope for the future.

For many years, his father's ring had served as a symbol for Cale. He had never admitted as much to himself, but now that the ring was gone, surrendered to a stupid bully on Tau-14, he felt the loss more sharply than he would have guessed. Maybe he needed a symbol after all, to remind him of who he was, what he wanted to be, what he was striving for.

After hours of agonizing, Cale finally fell into a deep, dreamless sleep. He was completely unprepared when Nikla came for them. The shaman looked deep into his eyes, studying him for a long moment, before making a musical trilling sound as if she approved of what she saw there. "No hurry, young one. You have done well. Please, refresh yourself. Today I shall introduce you to our government's leaders. Rontlyn the Great has a gift to offer you, Cale Tucker."

Pondering what kind of present the Qu'utians might want to give him, Cale retreated to the indicated cubicle, finding several oddly shaped holes in the floor and wall, and a meter-wide waterfall that occupied one corner of the high room. It took less than two minutes for Cale to wash himself clean in the sparkling warm water. As he stepped out of the waterfall, a bank of dryers in the wall activated. He was standing in the warm breeze when Tek entered.

"Please hold this." Tek handed him a padbook. Cale glanced at it, noting that it was a biography of Alanth the Great. The Vusstran scientist occupied himself at one of the holes in the wall, then shuffled back to Cale and spoke in a stage whisper. "That one, and that one." He pointed to one hole in the wall and another one in the floor.

Cale handed the padbook back to Tek. "Gotcha." Tek nodded absently and left the room, already absorbed in the biography.

Cale joined the others a few minutes later, feeling like a new Human. The four took individual balloon transports, Nikla leading the way. The shaman used a password to enter a long tube with a wind current that blew them along the passageway until they emerged into a brightly lit compound, at the center of which stood a building shaped like an inverted steeple.

Nikla touched down lightly on a broad, green field at the base of the building and released her balloon. Feet firmly planted, Cale let go of his balloon and looked around. The compound, hundreds of meters across, was encircled by a sturdy, impenetrable fence.

"Hey, is that spikevine?" Cale said.

The shaman nodded, pleased that he had noticed. "And our governmental building is shaped like the Sword of Alanth."

"Of course," Tek exclaimed.

Iji bounced up and down. "So you're saying this whole place is like a giant Qu'utchaa."

Tek had many new insights into Alanth after reading his biography, and he conversed amiably with Nikla as she led them into the building and past several checkpoints to the upper administration levels. There, a Qu'utian stood up quickly from behind a broad, glossy desk. "We are—are honored, Shaman Nikla, by your presence."

"Please tell Rontlyn the Great that her visitors are here to see her."

The receptionist disappeared through an inverted, triangular door. Within a moment, he returned and bowed. "If you'll follow me." He took them up one floor to an octagonal room lined on all sides by windows with intricately faceted bezels. A triangular table with a Qu'utchaa at its center was spread with a lush feast. Near one of the eight walls, on a raised dais, sat several official-looking Qu'utians.

Rontlyn the Great stood from her dais, introduced herself, and stepped lightly down to embrace Nikla. "And what have you to tell us, my faithful friend?" The leader looked warily at Cale and his companions. Cale noticed the symbol of Qu'utchaa engraved delicately into the skin of one of her hands.

"We can trust them," Nikla answered simply. "As I told you, the Human shares much of our pain. His world and his people also suffered under the Drej."

"That's all I needed to know," Rontlyn said, whirling toward her guests. "Now, won't you join us in breaking your fast?" She glanced up at her ministers and brusquely presented them. "Come, come, come. We haven't got all day."

During the sumptuous meal, Cale continued to wonder what the great leader wanted to give him. Iji conducted an animated conversation with several of the ministers, who seemed to be enjoying the precocious child's company. Tek, meanwhile, waxed eloquent about how inspirational he found the Qu'utian culture.

Finally, when there was a lull in the conversation, Rontlyn stood and commanded everyone's attention.

"Cale Tucker, fellow victim of the Drej, you and your people share a bond with all Qu'utians. We wish to offer you hope, to give you our symbol of strength."

Everyone at the table looked toward Cale, and he flushed.

Rontlyn the Great continued, "Your planet was destroyed by the Drej, just as Qu'ut Prime was. Often, when people are faced with such enormous problems, they surrender too easily. But you, Cale, must not surrender. You can also achieve victory through persistence, as the Qu'utians have."

She pointed spidery fingers toward the sword-and-spikevine symbol that ornamented the triangular table. "That is why we would like to offer you a Qu'utchaa. If you wear it on your skin, it will remind you to become stronger and never allow your spirit to be defeated." She turned her hand toward Cale to display the sword-and-spikevine design on it.

Cale wasn't sure how to respond. "You want to give me . . . a tattoo?"

"Yes. If you accept our gift, we are prepared to give it." Rontlyn flashed a glance at the shaman.

Nikla nodded. "I have my equipment with me." She looked from Rontlyn to Cale. "This is a great honor."

Still uncertain, Cale saw Tek give him a sober nod of encouragement. Iji grinned. "Good idea! It'll break up the monotony of your skin."

Rontlyn turned back to Cale. "If you agree, the ceremony will be in one hour."

Cale hadn't envisioned anything quite this complicated, nor had he imagined there would be so many spectators.

He had also expected to be standing, not lying on a sword-shaped wedge of polished rock set into the cavern floor at the center of a circle etched to look like spike-vine.

But the Qu'utians took this very seriously.

Cale had chosen to have the tattoo on his right, upper arm. Tek and Iji stood along the left side of the stone slab, the shaman on his right. Rontlyn stood at the head on a raised platform and spoke to the gathered crowd.

"Our people have learned victory through persistence," the leader said. "From us, these visitors have learned the same lesson, and we share it freely. From this day forward, our people will be allies of the heart with the Vusstrans Tek and Iji, and the Human Cale."

"Wow, some of them are crying," Iji whispered as she looked at the crowd.

"All this for a tattoo?" Cale whispered back. He wore close-fitting pants and a skintight, sleeveless shirt, leaving his feet, arms, and head bare.

Now Nikla spoke. "The Qu'utchaa is not to be worn lightly. Young Cale, do you understand and accept the meaning of the symbol?"

"Yeah . . . I do," Cale answered.

"You will become wise and strong in your time. This will not come without work, however. It will take many years, but yours is an important destiny, and this symbol is an important first step. Remember the truth my people have learned. It is why we have survived. Never accept defeat. The only true defeat comes in allowing your spirit to be conquered. Victory comes through persistence."

Cale felt as if he had been waiting all his life to hear

these words. He was no longer confused or embarrassed by all their attention. This was important. This was something he wanted.

"I will learn," he answered in a loud, confident voice. "I'll remember. I'll grow strong." He glanced up at Tek and Iji. His foster father and pod-sister fairly beamed with pride.

"Very well." The shaman held the laserscriber high over her head as if in benediction, then lowered it to her chest and folded both hands around it. "Victory, courage, persistence. These are not things we can give. We offer this symbol for you to wear as a reminder of the qualities to which we—and now *you*—aspire. Because you have willingly chosen to accept the Qu'utchaa, you must also participate in the process."

Cale lifted his left hand to clasp both of the shaman's hands in his, then pressed the laserscriber to his right arm. "This is my choice," he said.

–10–

After the tattoo work was finished, the ethereal aliens all paid homage to Cale. Heads down, they filed past Cale in the ceremonial chamber, then out into the open grotto again, looking up at the distant stone ceiling.

As the bustle diminished, Cale considered the new design still stinging on his arm. He could feel the flesh tingling as if in an effort to accept the Qu'utchaa imprinted there. A sword surrounded by a barbed ring.

Victory through persistence.

These survivors of a world-wrecking Drej attack had begun teaching Cale to think in new ways, to consider possibilities beyond simple acceptance of defeat. Too often he had grumbled and complained about his life. Perhaps Sam Tucker had been on the right track with his crazy dreams about humanity after all. . . .

He saw Iji staring at him with a strange look on her face, a mixture of awe and worshipfulness. His little pod-sister's hero worship had always been annoying, and now he didn't know how to live up to the kid's expectations. "What are you looking at, Ijit?" he said.

Instead of being insulted, Iji just grinned, then turned up her snout and flared her nose-slits at him.

Perhaps Tek had been right to take Cale out and away from Vusstra so that he could see new things. Unfortunately, after his encounter with Klegg on Tau-14 and losing his father's ring, Cale wasn't overly impressed with his fellow Humans. But maybe other civilizations in the Spiral Arm offered something worth seeing.

Sitting up, Cale rubbed the tingling skin on his triceps, twisting his neck to see the pattern. Tek looked at the young man with pride and approval, nodding somberly. . . .

At that moment, all the alarms started ringing. Blaring sounds echoed from the rock ceiling, shattering the reverent mood in the ceremonial chamber. Hooting sirens sent a ripple through the underground population. The remaining few Qu'utians moved about in a flurry, then fled the ceremonial chamber.

Rontlyn the Great rushed off with her advisors, sparing only a brief glance at Cale and the two Vusstrans. The tall, silvery-green shaman gestured hurriedly toward her guests. "Come. Join me in the observation sphere." Her bony elbows jutted upward as if she were ready to pounce. "We must see how dangerous this is." She strode out, leaving Tek, Cale, and Iji to hurry after her.

Inside the grotto, the Qu'utians moved like an army. Earlier, while the aliens had been going about their daily lives, their hidden world had seemed peaceful, a sheltered paradise with propeller kites and waterfalls and crystal fountains. Now though, they were a city under siege. All of the bone-thin aliens seemed to know their duties and set about them with intense determination.

"What is it? What's going on?" Cale jogged to keep up with Nikla's long strides. Intent on the emergency, the shaman wasted no time keeping her visitors in tow, nor did she answer him.

Finally, they reached the opening of a tall organpipe building that rose almost to the cave ceiling. Its top was crowned by a broad sphere studded with opaque crystal sheets. Several Qu'utians had already dashed inside.

Nikla stopped at the hatch and spun about, her purple eyes flaring with accusation. "Are you sure you weren't followed? Did you lure ships here?"

Tek blinked his round yellow eyes in surprise. "Why, no! Of course we were alone."

Cale broke in. "Hey, we barely made it through that asteroid field ourselves. There certainly wasn't anyone sneaking behind us."

After studying them, Nikla finally bobbed her head in resignation. "An emergency was declared by our surface teams." The shaman looked at the rock ceiling high above. "The dwellers in our ruined city have detected Drej ships—a fleet of Stingers is coming. It is well that we chose to hide the ship you came in."

Cale swallowed hard as they stepped inside the cylindrical building. The interior was hollow, like a giant reed, with living quarters built along the thick walls, and curved balconies inside the shaft's interior as well as outside.

Green balloons powered by propellers and lighter-than-air gas floated up the center of the shaft, while others drifted down after achieving a new equilibrium. Cale watched a succession of balloons rising and sinking, like a fireman's brigade of bright baubles.

Nikla said, "Grab a balloon and follow me. We must get to the top of the observation dome. Hurry!"

The shaman snagged the lower ring of a large balloon rising from below. The drifting sphere paused in midair, then its propeller picked up speed to lift her off the high ledge, carrying Nikla into the center of the tube.

"This doesn't look like a good idea to me," Cale said. "Aren't there stairs we could take? Or an elevator?"

"What's that extinct Earth bird you were telling me about, Cale?" Iji said. "Oh, that's right. *Chicken!*" She sprang out and grabbed the next balloon, then giggled as it carried her higher, swaying from side to side.

Nikla had already floated several body lengths upward. She released the suspension ring with one hand and gestured sharply for Cale and Tek to follow. Not willing to be outdone by his pod-sister, Cale grabbed the next balloon; Tek followed him.

After the first few seconds, he enjoyed the sensation of being aloft. Numerous balconies of the interior dwelling units were close enough that if he tilted the balloon and swung toward the wall, he could easily have let go of the balloon and landed inside someone's apartment.

Iji kicked her feet and laughed as she swayed, causing her balloon to rock from one side of the shaft to the other. Tek hung his arm over the ring, secured himself, and enjoyed the ride.

Alarms continued to rattle Cale's ears, echoing off the central shaft of the tube building. Qu'utians scurried about, some grabbing upward transport balloons, others rushing to balconies to snag descending balloons, riding all the way down to the bottom.

When the sirens and bells fell silent, Cale thought the emergency must have been declared over. Then sets of silent lights began to flash, and he realized that the Qu'utian underground city had entered an even higher state of alert, something so serious they didn't dare to generate a sound.

The balloons took them into an opening on the lower curve of the spherical observation dome. As Cale floated up through the floor, interior currents swirled them around to one side. He released his grip and dropped to the floor of the dome, landing among Qu'utians who operated the controls inside the main landing command center. Rontlyn the Great was already there, in charge of the operations.

Cale saw that the numerous crystal sheets studding the curved surface of the sphere were not windows after all, but screens that transmitted images from the wounded surface, the starry, meteor-studded sky, or the burned-out skyscrapers that had been smashed by the rubble of Qu'ut Prime.

The primitive upper inhabitants scurried about like shadows. They sounded their own whistling alarms and extinguished dim fires in the gaping, broken-mouthed openings of toppled structures.

Speaking in their melodious private language, the Qu'utians manned control boards, shifting images from the remote viewing windows. They panned up from the refugees' lockdown preparations, then centered on bright lights in the sky. The blips moved in a straight line, cutting across the asteroid field until they became discernible as a fleet of sharp-edged Drej Stingers. The scout ships glowed blue in the night sky, pulsing with ominous energy, like anger trapped in a bottle of lightning.

"Here they come," Nikla whispered.

Inside the observation dome, a hush fell over the Qu'utians. Workers shifted the transmitted views and increased magnification on individual Stingers until the images showed every ominous aspect of their appearance. To Cale, the vessels looked like rearing spiders. Under high magnification, the ships tore across the field of view, images grainy with atmospheric distortion.

"Now it is time to see if we have succeeded in playing dead. If the Drej think we remain crushed and defeated, we are of no concern to them." Nikla crossed her lanky arms over her chest.

"Why are we whispering?" Cale said, instinctively keeping his voice low. "We're underneath a mile of surface crust."

The shaman nodded. "Yes . . . but these are the *Drej*."

Iji drew a quick gasp as the Stingers on the screen altered their course in a single movement and swooped over the battered buildings. Seven scout ships cruised low over the burned metropolis, scanning to detect any evidence of civilization, any continued threat. The Drej played a glowing blue light, an unearthly sensor beacon, over the rubble.

Shadowy figures of the surface-dwelling Qu'utians ran for shelter, and the Stingers shot deadly destructive beams into the intact buildings, exploding walls, collapsing girders. More memories of the Qu'utian surface civilization fell into heaps of blasted stone.

The observers inside the underground dome gasped, but they could do nothing to help the martyred Qu'utians who had remained above to continue the ruse. Nikla huddled in tense despair, holding her breath and waiting to see what the Drej would do next.

The Stinger fleet circled again and made a slow sweep. Even this far below the ground, Cale imagined he could feel the humming of their engines, the throb of relentless power as they hovered low. They flew over the city a final time, and more energy beams lanced out to blast the fallen statue into shards of blackened gravel.

The Stingers blew up three other empty buildings on their way out. Then, their mission accomplished—presumably having found nothing on Qu'ut Minor to warrant their attention—the Drej fleet converged and shot upward into the sky. The pulsing blue ships streaked toward the asteroid belt, beyond which their Mothership no doubt waited in safety.

The Qu'utians in the observation dome leaned back with pronounced whistles and sighs of relief, but their celebration was tainted and subdued. The tall shaman ruffled the silvery-green growths of moss on her smooth skin and made a clicking noise. "Success. We have fooled the Drej." She sighed and strutted about the observation deck.

The viewing windows scanned to show images of surface dwellers crawling out of the debris, emerging from protected hiding places, and racing toward the burning wreckage of the newly demolished structures to search for survivors in the rubble.

More transport balloons waited, hanging at the ceiling of the observation dome. The shaman went to the opening and summoned an aide. "We must arrange for rescue parties. We will honor our martyrs before continuing research on how to destroy the Drej. But first," she said with a trilling, sad whistle, "we must recover and bury our dead."

−11−

"That was really creepy," Iji said with a shudder.

Inside the observation dome, the Qu'utians sent out tentative scans, confirming that the alien scout fleet had indeed departed from the system.

Cale stood in shock from what he had seen, shaking his head. "I watched the Drej blow up Earth when I was five years old, but that was so long ago, it's like remembering a nightmare. This feels so . . . real."

"The Drej are very real, young one," Nikla said.

From her command podium, Rontlyn the Great spoke in a low voice. "That is why the three of you must keep our secret."

"We will keep your trust," Tek answered, "but I'm afraid we must leave here at once."

"Don't forget, we don't like the Drej any more than you do," Iji piped up. "Right, Cale?"

"Yeah, well, about keeping your secrets?" Cale brought up a thought that had been nagging at the back of his mind. "Aren't you worried that my tattoo might somehow tip off the wrong people?" He looked down and swallowed hard. "If you think I might be a danger to you, maybe you should just cut this Qu'utchaa off my arm—"

"Oh, child!" the shaman broke in, a mixture of horror and amusement in her voice. "That will not be necessary."

"It comforts us to know the sacrifice you are willing to make on our behalf," Rontlyn said in a grave voice. "However, wearing the Qu'utchaa will never endanger us. Our race did not adopt that symbol until after the Drej went dormant. Since then, we have been sending out spies, smugglers, and traders to other planets to bargain for the supplies we need in rebuilding. We have even entered candidates in the Fauldro Flight Academy, so we can have qualified pilots to negotiate the hazardous asteroid field."

The shaman spread her hands in an isn't-it-obvious gesture. "Outsiders tend to draw their own conclusions when they see a sword and a coil of razorwire."

"Ah, I take your point," Cale said.

"So you're sure you don't have to slice off his arm?" Iji said with mock disappointment, then giggled. "I'm sorry, Cale. I'm glad you can keep the Qu'utchaa. I wouldn't have wanted you to lose both your symbols of hope."

Cale's stomach clenched. He hoped Tek wouldn't notice Iji's slip, but the Vusstran scientist turned toward him quickly. "What symbol did you lose?"

Cale and Iji spoke at the same time. "Nothing," he said.

"The ring," she said.

Tek wavered, blinked several times. His mouth opened and closed, but he said nothing. For the first time, he noticed that Cale no longer wore Sam Tucker's ring on his finger. "That ring was important, Cale. You don't understand how important."

Rontlyn's face suddenly became severe. "It was a symbol to you, yet you were careless enough to lose it?"

Cale nodded uncomfortably. "I'd rather not talk about it."

Iji jumped to his defense. "He didn't just lose it. A big bully on Tau-14 threatened to kill me. Cale gave him the ring to save my life."

While Tek looked very agitated, Rontlyn's face softened. "What did the ring mean to you?"

"My father gave it to me, so I guess it reminds me of him and all the things we used to do together, inventing stuff . . ."

"Anything else?" Nikla prompted.

Embarrassed by the sudden focus of attention, Cale fumbled for words. "I, uh, guess it was a reminder of my planet all in one piece."

"And good Humans who try to do good things," Iji supplied helpfully. "Not bullies like Klegg."

Cale glowered at Iji, wishing he hadn't been put on the spot like this. He'd been planning to tell Tek about losing the ring—when the time was right, of course.

Tek hung his head in distress. "It was hope for the future of humanity."

"Hey, let's not get carried away," Cale said.

But Rontlyn the Great focused on Tek's remark.

"Then the ring must be retrieved." Her tone brooked no argument.

The shaman placed a broad, spidery-fingered hand on Cale's tattoo. "Both symbols are important. Just as we rebuilt after the attack of the Drej, making ourselves strong from the inside, so you must rebuild." She placed her other hand to his chest. "From the inside. Get your ring back."

"But—it's not that simple," Cale said.

"The work of reclaiming what is ours is never easy," Rontlyn replied.

Iji interrupted, "Klegg said he came from a Human Drifter colony called New Marrakech. They were just on Tau-14 trading for spare parts."

The Vusstran scientist straightened. "Hmm, yes. I have all the known Drifter colonies marked on the new navigation charts that came with our TR-Epsilon Z. And the name New Marrakech sounds very familiar. Perhaps I knew one of the Humans who relocated there." He pondered a moment. "As part of Cale's 'group education,' I had planned to take him to a Drifter colony, let him meet more Humans and see how they live." Tek nodded, coming to a final decision. "I know where our next stop will be."

Tek was more disturbed than he could ever let Cale know. The fact that Sam Tucker had made Cale's ring meant it was special, but there was more to it than that. While Tek was still working on Earth, after agreeing to take Cale if any emergency should arise, Sam Tucker had said to Tek, "The ring is finished. If we're forced to separate, I'll give it to Cale. But make sure he never loses it. It's important."

And Tek had promised. Tek never broke a promise.

The Qu'utians provided the three travelers with everything they would need for the journey. Rontlyn the Great herself, her ministers, and the shaman all showed up to see the ship off.

They stood in the ruined surface city as dawn light broke over the devastated landscape. Rescue crews had finished their work retrieving bodies, putting out fires, tending injuries. Debris falling inside the building that had hidden their TR-Epsilon Z had scratched the hull, but caused no serious damage. Cale emerged from the cockpit after checking the systems and gave a thumbs-up to Tek. Luckily, the Stingers had not directly targeted the building that held the classic vessel.

The surface-dwelling Qu'utians had not been as fortunate, however. Seventeen had died in the offhand Drej attack. The sour smell in the air was worse.

"You have raised the young ones well," Nikla assured Tek as they stood in front of the ship. The tall, ethereal shaman bent to Iji and hugged her. "You will be a great one yourself one day. Rontlyn has told me this." Moving to Cale, she touched his tattoo one last time. "Always remember."

"I will," Cale said.

"As will I," Tek added. He looked at Cale and Iji with pride as they entered the spaceship.

"Well, it would be kind of hard to *forget*," Iji observed while Tek secured the hatch. "You know, we never gave our new ship a name."

"It wasn't exactly on the top of our list of priorities," Cale pointed out.

"We still need a name," Iji insisted.

"Okay, how about the *Ijit*?"

"What if we call it the *Dumb Big Brother*?"

Tek smiled to himself and hurried to the pilot's seat. Cale plopped down beside him at the copilot's station. "A ship's name is supposed to be something significant to the owner," Tek said.

"Oh? And what did the *Ale Keg* mean?" Cale asked.

"I didn't name that ship," Tek said defensively.

"How about the *Lost Ring*?" Iji said.

Tek strapped himself in and fired up the ship's engines, preparing to leave the system. "We hope the ring will not be lost for long."

"The *Qu'utchaa*?" she asked.

"Too dangerous," Cale pointed out. "Too specific to the Qu'utians."

"Then how about the *Sword Ring*?" Iji asked. "You know, like in the Qu'utchaa, but it could remind you of the sword on your arm and the ring that we're going to get back. It has meaning, you know."

"It has a *ring* to it," Cale quipped.

"Well, *sword* of," Iji shot back.

Tek smiled as they continued to bicker. It was good to be with his family.

−12−

As they left the Qu'utians and their underground secret behind, rising above the scarred world, Cale sat
in his uncomfortable copilot's seat, pondering what he
had seen and discovered there. The cockpit of the TR-
Epsilon Z seemed quiet and somber.

Tek set their flight protocol and headed again toward
the dangerous rubble field along the orbit of Qu'ut
Prime. Cale looked down and watched the ruined cities
vanish in the distance. "It's tough to believe that
Qu'utians don't know why the Drej picked them out of
all the races in the Spiral Arm," he said. "Hardly makes
sense."

Tek shook his head. "Hmm, no. No more sense than
choosing Earth. We are all aliens to each other . . . but
the Drej are more alien than any of us." The Vusstran
scientist heaved a great sigh. "I respected your father's
dreams. Sam Tucker dreamed of restoring life where it

had once been, creating an Eden in a harsh or dying environment . . . like my own planet.

"That's why I worked with him, why I agreed to take you under my care when he had to leave, on the day the Earth died. Sam Tucker's dreams were larger than most people could carry alone. And that"—his voice grew harder and sterner—"is why we have to get your ring back."

Cale's heart sank. "We'll never find it again."

Iji came forward, chastising him with her piping voice. "Didn't the Qu'utians teach you anything about victory through persistence?" His pod-sister's smooth forehead wrinkled in a perplexed frown. "I know all Humans look alike, but I'll never forget Klegg's ugly face."

"Your father meant for you to keep that ring." Tek played his clawed fingers over the control panels. "Once we get through the asteroid field, I'll set coordinates for New Marrakech. There's a man I'd like to see there, someone who worked on the Titan Project back on Earth. Besides, you should meet other Humans than just the bad examples you found on Tau-14. And you need to find your ring."

"If you say so," Cale replied, glum.

Tek turned around, giving Iji a stern look. "And *you*, pod-daughter, must soon return home to Vusstra and your group school where you belong." Iji pouted and her skin turned darker colors.

Ahead, the asteroid field looked like a handful of rocks flung at them. The rubble drifted about in erratic orbits that had not yet stabilized since the Drej destruction of Qu'ut Prime. Cale thought of them as teardrops of stone, grieving for the fall of the Qu'utian civilization.

"Can we'll just follow our same course out?" Cale asked, but as he watched the shifting, zero-gravity avalanche drifting along, he already knew the answer. "Ah, right—no stable path."

Tek explained. "Within a few millennia, this asteroid belt will have settled down enough that daring navigators—or maybe some of those crack Qu'utian pilots being trained on Fauldro—can plant marker buoys for a route to Qu'ut Minor. But it has been only four decades. For now, we'll just have to be daredevils."

"I hope these asteroids managed to smash one or two of the Drej Stingers on their way out," Iji said with a huff.

"I doubt we'd have such luck," Cale muttered. Absently, he rubbed the new tattoo on his arm, which still stung. He had a feeling it would be sore for days.

"Hang on," Tek said with only a slight tremor in his normally good-humored voice. "Time to dodge rocks again."

The ship dove into the asteroid storm. Tek gripped the *Sword Ring*'s controls, swung their vessel from side to side, plunging through the obstacle course. He squinted, as if he didn't want to see what lay ahead.

Cale leaned back in the misshapen chair, pressing his feet against the deck and clenching white-knuckled fists around imaginary controls. "Do you want me to fly, Tek? I can do this."

"No, thank you, Cale," Tek said, terrified of the hazardous course, but more terrified to let his Human ward make the attempt.

As the *Sword Ring* passed through the shattered

world, Cale watched two meteoroids collide with each other. They broke apart and crumbled, grinding into smaller pieces of space gravel and dust. The ship looped over a rolling shard that, as it rotated, turned to display a vacuum-blasted graveyard that had once been a city. Tenuous gas hung around the larger chunks like a haze, slowly seeping into space.

Unseen, a blue light glimmered from behind an asteroid, and a single Drej Stinger activated its engines, streaking out after them . . . a member of the scout patrol left behind to watch for intruders.

A warning indicator on the TR-Epsilon Z's control panel blinked on. While Tek concentrated on flying through the hazardous corridor, Cale studied the sensor screen and turned pale. "We got company. Drej Stinger, right on our tail!"

"Vusstrans don't have tails," Iji said.

"It was lying in wait," Tek said. "But how could it have known about us?" Frowning, he increased his engine speed, though he was already having trouble maneuvering among the crashing meteoroids.

The Drej ship approached with streamlined ease—and opened fire. Blaster streaks creased the blackness in space, ricocheting off a hard metal lump from the core of Qu'ut Prime. The Drej shot again, scoring a black mark along the hull of the *Sword Ring*.

"They didn't even send a warning!" Iji cried. "They didn't even ask us to surrender."

"They're Drej," Cale said, as if that answered all of her questions.

As he flew, Tek's skin paled, making the dark

blotches more prominent, a sign of his anxiety. "A TR-Epsilon Z isn't a battleship."

"I'll take care of the shooting," Cale said. Though he wasn't any better at aiming than Iji or Tek, *someone* had to do this, and he still had his pride. He would draw a certain amount of satisfaction from blasting the aliens who had destroyed his beautiful Earth.

Cale shot twice, but the Stinger ship dodged easily, spinning without worrying about G-forces that would have killed a Human. Gritting his teeth, Cale continued to fire a constant stream. Through sheer luck, he managed to strike three grazing blows, leaving dark marks on the glowing blue energy of the Stinger hull.

But the pursuer did not slow, and the Drej had much better aim than Cale.

Tek raced toward the fringe of the asteroid field. The Stinger closed the distance, firing again. The *Sword Ring* rocked with the impact, and Tek frowned down at the status board. "A few more hits like that, and we'll have a hull breach."

"Then we'd better not let them hit us." Cale glanced through the kleersteel port, saw the clusters of rocks dissipating as they approached the boundary. "Don't fly *out* of the asteroids. Go there." He pointed forward. "Toward the denser part."

"Are you crazy?" Iji asked in alarm.

"Fly between those two big ones that are about to collide. We can leave him in the dust." Cale grinned down at the weapons controls. "And I'll make some more dust just to muddy his view."

Without questioning, Tek flew straight between the two moonlet-sized, rotating boulders. The Stinger in-

creased speed, but so did Tek, widening the gap. The
Sword Ring streaked through the closing separation,
barely scraping between the two rocks, leaving the alien
behind. When the meteoroids finally collided, Cale let
loose a full volley of his aft weapons. The heat blasted
the orbiting stones into thousands of flaming chunks that
flew in all directions, blinding the Drej sensors.

"Now, Tek! Shoot upward, straight out of the ecliptic,
the shortest distance that'll get us out of the asteroid
field."

"Hmm, yes. Good idea." Tek's clawed fingers flew
over the controls, and the powerful old ship changed
course by ninety degrees. They shot out of the asteroidal
orbit, leaving the Drej floundering below. "Now I'll set
a course for New Marrakech in the Solbrecht system.
Full speed." Tek punched their thrusters, and the *Sword
Ring* roared forward faster than the speed of light.

"Can he follow us now?" Iji asked, breathless.

"It's always possible, but I doubt we left enough of a
course signature," Tek said.

"Then again," Cale said, tightening his lips into a grim
line, "they're Drej."

They arrived, battered, but no worse for wear, in the
Solbrecht system and made their way toward the Drifter
colony. They were still too far away to see details of
New Marrakech, but the floating conglomeration of
cobbled-together refugee ships looked like a bright star
orbiting in a no-man's-land around the sun, encroaching
upon the territory of no alien race.

Humans had little prestige in the Spiral Arm, and certainly no clout. A few vagabond remnants of Cale's peo-

ple bounced from place to place, with no central home. No alien race would take them in and give the survivors a new planet. Someday, though, the Human race might find their own world.

"It doesn't look like too big of a place," Iji said, her face pressed to the kleersteel port. "We'll find your ring down there, Cale."

He just snorted, not willing to get his hopes up.

Just then the persistent Drej Stinger roared across their front bow, firing its weapons before they had even picked up its arrival on the sensor display.

"What?" Cale shouted.

"How did he follow us?" Iji wailed as she was thrown to the deck. She rolled against the bulkhead wall, holding her head. In reflex, Tek hauled back on the piloting controls, and the *Sword Ring* soared around in a backward loop while the Drej circled and came back for another shot at them.

Cale gasped as the blue streak roared in front of the cockpit, and he tried to get off a shot. Tek rolled their ship in what he thought was an evasive maneuver, but the Drej still hit them.

Alarms buzzed from the TR-Epsilon Z's strained systems.

So dizzy that he could barely see straight, Cale fired his weapons anyway. As the Stinger came around again, he noted black blotches on its glowing hull: this was the same vessel they had just fought in the asteroid field.

"It's going to destroy us," Tek said.

Cale squeezed his eyes shut and fired all the weapons in a fan pattern as the Drej came forward on a collision course, as if intending to ram their ship.

No one was more surprised than Cale when his shots locked on, and the blasts scored through the energy barrier and exploded the scout ship right in front of them.

"I did it!" Cale said. "I got it!"

Iji scrambled to her feet to throw her arms around Cale.

"Whoa!" Tek shouted, not sounding elated at all. His ship collided at full speed with the expanding debris cloud of the exploded Stinger.

Molten lumps of wreckage from the Drej vessel smashed into their hull. The Stinger debris remained solid long enough to cause impact damage, then dissipated into clouds of crackling energy, which blew out half of the *Sword Ring*'s control systems. Explosions pummeled their engines, weakening their defensive screens and cracking open the airtight seal in the cargo bay below.

"We're losing air!" Tek shouted. Cale, noting the location of the hull breach, punched buttons to seal off the cargo hold, praying that the door circuits remained functional. They didn't have anything valuable down in the hold, but he realized with a shudder of relief that when Iji had stowed away, she might well have thought to hide down there.

One of their engines shorted out and died while uneven thrust from the second one made their path corkscrew like a spitting string of firecrackers. Tek wrestled for control, and though their ship still bounced and shuddered, they began to crawl forward, injured and damaged.

But still alive.

The bright spot of the Drifter colony grew larger as

they limped toward it. Cale still felt an adrenaline rush from his recent battle, but he was not overly eager to be stuck in an entire colony full of homeless Humans.

"I just hope they know how to fix spaceships," he said.

– 13 –

The sparking, smoking *Sword Ring* limped toward New Marrakech, and Cale got his first good look. He wasn't sure what he had expected from a Drifter colony, but it sure wasn't this.

After seeing the miraculous underground city of the Qu'utians, this hodgepodge, tied-together "glob" of ramshackle Earth escape ships, supply haulers, storage units, and unrecognizable hunks of old machinery looked like an abomination to anyone with a sense of culture. On Tau-14, both ingenuity and careful consideration had been used to build and maintain the salvage station from recycled parts. Even the abandoned industrial works on Vusstra had more aesthetic appeal than New Marrakech.

Ten years ago, just before the imminent Drej attack, every possible escape craft and container had lifted into Earth orbit. Over the years, groups of those surviving ships had congregated in space like old-fashioned gypsy camps. Humans bound their vessels together and tried to make a home for themselves. *Drifter colonies.* But these ramshackle colonies had to bring in *all* of their outside resources, everything from power to water to air itself.

"Where exactly do you suppose the docking bays are?" Tek asked, squinting through the *Sword Ring*'s front viewports.

Cale grimaced. "Haven't got a clue."

"I'm trying to signal their docking control," Iji said, "but I'm not getting anything back." She sighed. "I'm afraid our comm unit is totally out."

Tek fired the engines briefly, using their scant remaining fuel vapors, and they Drifted closer to the colony. Then one of the engines sputtered, sending them into an uncontrollable spin.

Tek was flung from his chair. Iji squealed. Cale clung to the copilot's station with both hands. "Hey, whoa! Whoaaa!" The spinning ship turned space outside the viewport into a whirlpool of stars. The contents of his stomach—apparently dissatisfied with their current location—began a slow surge up his throat.

"Altitude control," Tek cried, tumbling through the cockpit past Cale.

"He means the jets," Iji yelled.

Fighting nausea, Cale fumbled with the navigation panel, searching for the right controls. *Spin. Whirl.* It was difficult to concentrate. He muttered out loud to keep his mind focused. "Let's see, we're spinning toward the right, which means I need to fire the—"

Pshht! The spinning slowed a bit. *Pshht!* Cale fired the attitude control jet again. The *Sword Ring* now entered a languorous spiral, still headed toward the Drifter colony. Tek thumped down, shook himself, and climbed back into the pilot's seat.

"Hmm, yes. Never forget to fasten your crash restraints," Tek said in a sheepish voice.

Cale grunted, then pointed toward the unappealing lumps of the colony cluster. "Those look like the docking ports over there. Wouldn't now be a good time to start aiming toward them?"

"Hmm, yes." Tek looked down at the controls with a perplexed frown. "It would be, if we had any fuel left. Doesn't look promising. Only fumes." He studied the cockpit for inspiration while Iji resumed trying to contact anyone at the colony.

"This is the *Sword Ring* to New Marrakech docks. *Sword Ring* to New Marrakech docks. Our ship is badly damaged. We're on a collision course with your docking bay and have lost all means of controlling our ship. Repeat: We have lost all attitude control," she said in a sweet voice.

Cale growled. "Uh, Tek? Normally I'd be the last person to say this, but aren't we going a bit f-f-fast?"

"Hmmm, exactly. Too fast. Yes, too fast," Tek mused.

"What about those?" Cale asked, pointing at a cluster of switches above Tek's head.

New Marrakech loomed even larger in their front viewports. Tek glanced at the switches with a frown of his fleshy lips. "Mechanical dispersal system, manually operated. Usually discharged toward the aft, but—" He twisted a dial and shook his head. "Goes against everything I was ever taught." He flicked a switch.

Tchoong. A compact projectile ejected in the forward direction, and the *Sword Ring* recoiled, slowing their forward momentum. The projectile then dispersed into space before reaching the Drifter colony.

Cale gave a sigh of relief. "Well, that slowed us down. Now if we could only steer. What was that, anyway?"

Tek shook his head sadly. "Such a waste. Our garbage. I had meant to recycle it, but when that Drej Stinger attacked, it slipped my mind."

"Think of it as fuel, Father," Iji said. "We used it to brake our speed, so it wasn't really wasted." Tek brightened.

"Uh, I hate to mention this," Cale said, "but if those are the docking bays . . . ?" He pointed to a broad, rectangular opening.

"Ah, yes!" Tek said, as if suddenly comprehending. "Then we will miss the opening by approximately five meters."

"Not to mention that we'll smash into a solid metal hull, and probably break up and be turned into space dust," Cale added. "I don't know why we thought these people were going to be able to help us. Their whole colony looks like some giant broken toy."

The *Sword Ring* drifted inexorably toward the colony's metal outer wall above the docking bay entrance.

"Don't forget, victory through persistence," Iji said in a singsong voice. "Strength through unity."

"What's the point in being unified with a bunch of incompetent losers?" Cale asked. "I bet they couldn't even—" The ship gave a jolt. "What the—"

The ship jolted again, stopped, then Drifted downward and began to glide soundlessly forward, precisely toward the center of the docking bay, where a connecting metal arm and an atmosphere ring reached out toward them.

"Tractor beam," Tek observed, sounding pleased and unsurprised. "That'll be very snug. Perfect."

Iji giggled. "Incompetent, huh, Cale?"

Cale muttered darkly, "I'm glad to see they can do *something* right."

The Drifter colony was nearly as disorganized inside as it had appeared from the outside. While Cale, Iji, and Tek assessed the damage the Drej Stinger had done, swarms of workers hurried in and out of the docking bay, each on some indecipherable errand.

Two hours passed in welding, patching, reassembling, clamping, and rerouting before Cale said what the three of them had already privately concluded. "We're going to need parts."

"Hmm, yes. Quite a few, it would seem," Tek said.

A short, balding man with flowing robes strode toward the three. "Welcome," he beamed. "I'm Dockmaster Blish. I trust you had a comfortable landing? We received your distress signal. Is there anything I can do to assist you? I can direct you to our best antique salvage yards. For such a classic spaceship, that would be the best place to begin your search."

They took a list of establishments from Dockmaster Blish, who looked delighted to have the business.

"We obviously won't be finishing our repairs today," Tek said after the man had strutted away. "I suggest we get started on our other business. I'd like to make a few inquiries, find out if your father's old friend is here, perhaps someone who also worked on the Titan Project."

"In that case, I'll go looking for the parts," Cale offered. "A thrust flux stabilizer for this old model is going to be hard to find."

"I thought you would try to look for your ring, as the Qu'utians suggested," Tek said.

"I will—at the same time that I'm hunting down the parts we need." Cale spread his hands as if to say, "See what a great idea this is?"

"I can go with Cale, then," Iji spoke up.

"No, you are going to stay here, Ijit. Keep an eye on the ship," Cale said sternly. "This is something I've got to do on my own."

Iji hugged her arms to her chest and pouted.

— 14 —

N ew Marrakech was nothing to brag about, as far as
  Cale was concerned. And the Drifters couldn't even
keep the place clean.

While Tek went off on his errand "to meet an old
Titan acquaintance," Cale wandered through the streets
and alleys. The inhabitants had done their best to re-
create a part of old Earth with exotic Moroccan and Arab
cultures, but New Marrakech welcomed everyone. Human survivors were too few to engage in old feuds and
rivalries. The refugees had come together with a common bond, each following their own religious and cultural practices.

Cale had used a few credits to buy a map of the
souks—the crowded bazaar of merchant stalls, tiny
dwellings, awnings, and food stands that were as scattered and disorganized as the asteroids in the belt around
Qu'ut Minor.

He saw women in lovely, colorful scarves and robes,

women with lush dark hair, women with mysterious black eyes—enough to make him dizzy. He had never seen so many female Humans before in his life—they seemed like alien creatures to him.

The smells of cinnamon and cardamom, roasting coffee and hot frying oil, made his mouth water. Tek had always given his foster son the bland Vusstran nourishment made from yeasts, algaes, and recycled proteins, so Cale had little experience with Earth cuisine. Stomach grumbling, he stepped under a red-and-white-striped awning where a man had set up a cooking stand on two rusty metal cargo barrels with an ionization solar heater for a hot plate. He sizzled cubes of marinated meat over the brazier and fried strongly seasoned couscous in a big pan.

The man was round-cheeked, with a large dimple in his chin. His eyebrows were even darker than his eyes, and he was quick to flash a smile as Cale sniffed appreciatively. "Very inexpensive, my young friend! You've never tasted the like."

"That's the truth," Cale admitted. Reaching into his pocket, he found a few of the small coins he'd gotten from Tek and bought a plateful of the food. He wolfed down the skewered meat, then a wedge of honey bread. Eating with his hand as the man instructed him, Cale scooped couscous into his mouth. He wasn't sure how to chew the tiny, grainy food, but mushed it around in his mouth, enjoying the taste.

He picked out a long scarlet pod from the couscous. "What's this?"

"It is delicious, my friend," the proprietor said.

Cale popped it into his mouth, bit down, then felt an

acid-hot explosion like lava on his tongue. He had swallowed too soon, and now the oily pepper pod burned all the way down his throat. His eyes watered and he gasped, fanning air into his mouth as if that would do any good.

The proprietor chuckled at his reaction. "Another piece of bread and something to drink will cost you extra, my friend."

Cale gladly handed over the last of his coins. He gulped down the bread and a sweet fruit soda that cleared his palate enough to make his eyes stop watering.

"You will learn to like the peppers if you try them again," the man said, but Cale didn't think he was ready for any such adventure in the near future.

He noticed the man's twisted neon sign, with its lacy Arabic lettering. The light flickered and buzzed as it struggled to remain illuminated. Breaking down . . . just like everything else on this Drifter colony.

Cale raised his eyebrows. "Why don't you fix that? It's embarrassing."

"Fix it?" the proprietor answered. "I have no spare parts."

"So I'm guessing you have no idea what's wrong with this sign. You don't *need* spare parts for this." Cale climbed onto the rickety stand, fiddled with the neon bulb contacts, electrical ballast, and power supply. Within seconds, the sign blazed a brilliant lavender.

The proprietor smiled even more broadly. "Wonderful. Wonderful. How did you do that?"

Cale rolled his eyes. It had been a simple repair.

"Here. I will give you a whole plateful of those red peppers you like so much."

The proprietor began scooping peppers onto a dish, but Cale raised his hands. "I think I'll pass." Before he could back away, Cale stopped. "I am looking for some information, though. Do you know where I can find a young man named Klegg?"

"Klegg." The man barely stopped himself from spitting into his own food. "What do you want with him?"

"I want to settle a score."

Now the man beamed. "Ah, so you *will* be wanting the peppers then." He offered a package of crumbled red pods to Cale, who took it dubiously. "These are dry, powdered peppers. Even hotter."

"What I really wanted was to know where to find Klegg."

The proprietor pursed his lips and noticed that Cale carried one of the electronic maps of the souks in New Marrakech. "I see you have a locator. May I?" He extended his tanned hand, and Cale gave him the device. The proprietor made *tsk*ing sounds. "Severely out of date. I hope you didn't pay too much for this."

"No wonder I was lost," Cale said.

"No, everyone gets lost. But you should at least have a good map." He punched in some updates by hand and highlighted a general area of the Drifter colony. "This is where that bully hangs out most often, not far from the spaceship mosque. You will find him. Be prepared." The man smiled. "Use my peppers."

Behind him in the souks, Cale heard a crash. Several monkeys escaped from cages, running loose. A vendor cursed, complaining about clumsiness, while his young boy helper raced off to catch the small animals. "You come back here!" The man shouted at someone else, and Cale caught a glimpse of what had to be a young Vus-stran girl.

Iji. The little pest was following him. He groaned, but didn't want to go rescue her. She had gotten into her own mess.

He trudged across the complicated maze of the souks, dodging customers who jostled and bounced against him. No doubt some of them were pickpockets, but Cale's pockets were empty anyway. Somewhere behind him, Tek's bothersome pod-daughter was probably following. If she was wandering around on her own, why couldn't she go look for the thrust flux stabilizer they needed to fix the TR-Epsilon Z?

Cale got lost several more times, but eventually managed to find the right way. Straight lines did not exist in the souks. He observed with scorn and disappointment how run-down the entire Drifter colony was. Everywhere he looked, instead of being proud of what they had and who they were, these refugees had put together conglomerations of buildings, old ships, and storage units—and then let them fall into disrepair. Didn't anyone know how to fix them? Couldn't they read their own technical manuals?

As he walked down the narrow, convoluted street, Cale spotted a sandal maker working at his table. A portable atmosphere pump whirred and hummed beside his door, spitting out warm dust as it circulated the air. People jostled by, covering their mouths and noses with scarves. The sandal maker had many items on display, but few customers were willing to stop and choke on the air next to his stall.

Cale frowned in disgust. "Why don't you just fix that thing so it stops spewing dust on everyone?"

The sandal maker looked at the young man, who was obviously not a native of New Marrakech. Grasping his tools, he raised a callused hand in a helpless gesture. "I don't have any parts to fix it, so I have no choice but to turn the generator like this until it breaks down. Otherwise, I have no cool air for the back of the shop where it gets hot."

Cale knelt beside the atmosphere pump and banged its housing. More dust poured out. He coughed and looked at the sandal maker, annoyed. "When's the last time you changed the filter?"

The craftsman gave him a blank look. "Changed the filter?"

Cale's shoulders slumped. "Do you at least clean it?"

The man's expression gave Cale his answer. Making a rude sound, he tore the cowling off and removed the filter, took it around back, where he battered and cleaned the thick mesh, knocking years' worth of dust and grime away. "You should soak this in a solvent to clean all of the gunk, but now it'll be a lot better."

The sandal maker's eyes gleamed. "This is wonderful. I thank you so much."

"You can thank me by giving me directions." He hauled out his map. "I'm lost. I'm trying to find . . ." He held out the lighted section.

The sandal maker grabbed the map pad out of his hand. "Worthless junk. Who sold you this?" He tossed it with a clatter into the back of the sandal shop.

"Hey, that's mine!"

"I will give you a good one." The sandal maker produced a folded paper map, hand drawn, showing streets and stalls. He circled the spaceship mosque, then took great care to mark in color numerous establishments. "These are my friends. They'll do good business for you."

"Unless they can find me a thrust flux stabilizer for a TR-Epsilon Z, I'm not interested," he said. "I'm just looking for . . ." He stopped himself. "Just looking for someone."

Cale took the new map, thanked the man, and set off on his new route between the ramshackle buildings around him. He could spend all day, every day, for the rest of his life, just taking care of what the Drifters had let fall into disrepair. He shook his head in disgust. "What is wrong with these people?"

When Tek finally located the address of a man he had not seen in ten years, he ducked under a low overhang. Instead of a door, the opening had been covered with silk curtains and beads.

"Hello? Mohammed Bourain?" Tek called into dimness. He heard classical music of a kind he hadn't experienced since the destruction of Earth. A Human composer named Mozart, he believed. He smelled incense, saw candles. "I hope that you will remember me."

Inside, a tall man with dark hair, aquiline nose, and bronze skin moved forward. The crow's-feet around his eyes implied that he spent a lot of time thinking and remembering, but when he saw the face of the Vusstran at his door—a strange sight indeed on a Drifter colony— the man, Mohammed, brightened.

"Tek! Why, of course I remember you. You worked with Sam Tucker. We spent many months together, though our work on *Titan* didn't often intersect. I was more interested in . . . cultural preservation." He clasped Tek's hand and shook it vigorously. "Come in. Come into my dwelling, please." Mohammed made Tek sit down on a soft camel-leather ottoman. Intricate designs had been carved and scrolled into the surface.

Tek sniffed the strange aromas, gazed around at the exotic decorations. "I've come to talk to you about the Titan Project. We are on New Marrakech to make ship repairs, and I remembered hearing that you were here." He spread his broad palms. "I hope you can help me."

"Of course, of course," Mohammed said. "But first, let us have tea." He went through an elaborate cere-mony, preparing dried leaves in a mixture of boiling sugar water. "No fresh mint, I'm afraid. My greenhouse garden . . . well, I got too distracted with other work. I forgot to water it. And my son Ishaq is not good at remembering things either. He always has his nose in a book."

"This will be fine." Tek took a tiny sip of the brew, not certain whether or not it might be toxic to his spe-cies. "You remember that I was working with Sam Tucker on the Titan eco-restoration work?"

Mohammed slurped his tea and gave a long sigh of satisfaction. "Yes, I remember. Environmental remedi-ation, planetary reconstruction."

"I called it *healing*," Tek said. "And my own world of Vusstra is in great need of such healing. I studied with Sam Tucker, and when the Drej destroyed Earth, he flew off in the *Titan* himself. I took what I could, but now that I'm trying to reproduce the final stages of his work, I am missing important information about the catalyst to the process."

"Well, the technical details were beyond me." Mohammed took another drink of his tea. He tilted the pot to refill Tek's glass, though the Vusstran had barely sipped from it. "I am not certain anyone but Sam Tucker—anyone of *any* species—could understand all the details of his work."

"Oh, I understand them well enough," Tek said without any modesty whatsoever. "At least the parts in my possession. But I am missing vital information. I want to use a Titan process to add a new spark of life to my weary planet. Do you keep any records? You escaped in a different ship. Did you bring any of Sam Tucker's background information with you?"

"Records?" The tall, dark man beamed a huge smile at Tek. "Archiving information was my first and most important love. Of course I have records. All of them, I believe."

Tek's yellow eyes widened into large circles. "If I had that information, I could turn Vusstra green and healthy again."

Mohammed stood up and smiled. "Then, my friend, you must have what you need."

– 15 –

For as long as Iji could remember, she had been good at hiding—and not always to cause mischief, of course. Sometimes she watched her pod-father at work, careful not to disturb him, but most of the time she liked to keep an eye on Cale. He got annoyed whenever he caught her watching, so she had learned to become stealthy over the years.

And staying out of sight here on New Marrakech was much easier than on Vusstra.

Atmosphere fields shimmered overhead, letting starlight through, diluted by the glow of artificial sunshine. Sections of the Drifter colony had remarkably different architectures, because of the wide variety of vessels that the refugees had fused together to make this temporary world. Iji smelled the usual chemicals and industrial scents of atmosphere processors and recyclers, of course, but New Marrakech also carried a heady blanket of Human aromas—their homes, their clothes, their food. The buildings were close together, far more crowded than anything she had seen on Vusstra. Though she was an alien, the Humans paid no special attention to her.

Cale didn't seem to notice all the marvelous details as he marched through the convoluted souks, intent on his mission. Iji suspected he *knew* she was there, somewhere behind him. He hadn't really expected her to stay at the ship, had he? They had work to do, and she wanted to get even with Klegg as much as Cale did.

Iji admired her pod-brother and tried to imitate him, partly because Tek had told many stories about Sam Tucker and partly because, well, Cale fascinated her. She wanted to fix and invent things the way he did. She wanted to seem bold and fearless like him.

Because of their polluted world, most Vusstrans spent their time inside climate-controlled cermet buildings. But Cale liked to wander off by himself, saying it reminded him of the good parts of being a kid. She realized that Cale was trying to figure out who he was and what he wanted to do with the rest of his life. In fact, she probably understood her pod-brother even better than Tek did. Iji often followed him at a distance, across the wilderness, as when he'd gone to the mudpots.

Now, she mirrored his movements in the discreet way she'd taught herself. When he stopped at salvage piles to rummage through old parts, Iji halted twenty meters away and looked for parts, too. She pawed through tangles of snapbrackets, load-adjusters, grav-simulator boxes, megacircuit clusters, antique vocal modulators, broken scutbots, and parts whose function she could not begin to guess.

Cale muttered, kicked a pile, and moved on. Iji followed him.

The souks were so crowded, the stalls so rickety, that Iji had inadvertently upended a pottery display, unleashed several pet monkeys, and gotten dirty footprints on beautiful faux-silk scarves and cotton djellabas that had been on display. Fortunately, nothing was broken or permanently stained: Iji had righted the damage as much as possible and hurried on her way.

She spent hours trailing Cale through corridors and alleys and sealed field domes. Cale had just disappeared behind a metal bulkhead, and Iji was planning to let him get some distance ahead before she followed him through the doorway, when she heard his voice and others—all Human—followed by a loud, sneering catcall.

To her dismay, she recognized one voice instantly: Klegg.

Cale let the sandal maker's hand-drawn map fall to the metal floorplates of the New Marrakech "street." He had found what he was looking for.

"Well, whaddya know," Cale said. "Right where I expected you to be."

Klegg and his lieutenants stood together, looking for trouble and very surprised to find Cale. Even after the Tau-14 incident, Cale felt strange to be surrounded by Humans every direction he turned. The bullies had never expected to see him again.

Unfortunately, during his long search through the souks, Cale had been more interested with finding Klegg than with formulating his plan. Sure, he intended to negotiate—that had been the idea, anyway—but he hadn't actually figured out what line of reasoning or form of barter would convince Klegg to give the ring back. Now he would have to think fast.

"Well, if it isn't the junior crackpot," Klegg said, a slow smile spreading across his lean face. He nudged the nearest bully, Blitz, who dutifully laughed.

Standing in the close, narrow street, Cale fixated immediately on the golden ring, which hung from a chain around the wiry youth's neck. He found himself wondering why Klegg had not simply traded it away for a more useful item.

"I see you noticed my trophy," the bully said, glancing down at the ring, toying with it. He also wore a new rainbow-silk shirt, since Iji had torn his other one. "What brings you to our colony, Tucker? Visiting relatives?"

"Maybe he came to arrange a betrothal," Blitz said. "He's about the right age."

Klegg chuckled out loud, an unpleasant-sounding laugh. "In that case, I'll bet he has plenty of credits with him this time."

Cale straightened and spoke in what he hoped was a calm, commanding voice. "I came here for my ring."

Klegg's smile became a wolfish grin. "So, you did bring credits, then. It's going to cost you. Plenty."

Cale said, "I hoped we could negotiate more of a—"

"Maybe you were planning to trade us the little Vusstran girl? She might make a good enough servant around our headquarters," Klegg said.

"Sorry, I didn't bring along any children for you to torture this time." Anger and frustration welled up inside Cale. "Last I heard, slavery was illegal in this system."

Klegg shrugged one shoulder, not bothering to listen any further. "Take him, boys. We can have some fun."

"What?" Cale said. "You want to risk your new rainbow-silk shirt?"

The wiry ringleader crossed both arms over his chest while the others sprang at Cale and pummeled him with fists, elbows, knees, and pointed boots.

"Bring him to headquarters," Klegg said, "where we can have a little more privacy."

Cale was breathing in gasps when Blitz and another bully picked him up, one by each arm, and began dragging him between them. Groggy and aching, Cale remembered little of the trip until Blitz and his companion tossed him unceremoniously onto the hard deckplates of a large cylindrical chamber.

He groaned and decided he should have come up with an actual *plan*, instead of trusting his wits. This wasn't turning out as well as he'd hoped. Before he could open his swollen eyes, a pitcher of cold water splashed across his face and chest. Right now the sensation was welcome. He sat up with a start, only to be confronted with Klegg, who squatted in front of him.

"What do you think of our new headquarters?" he said, indicating the armor-walled chamber. "Part of a hollowed-out reactor core from a derelict ship. We got it on Tau-14, brought it back here. So it's a recent addition."

Cale glanced around the hollow reactor vessel, then shook his head to clear it. "Seems . . . very appropriate," he observed. "Though you might look more at home in a trash-compactor pod."

Klegg put his fists on his hips. "Seal the blast doors, Blitz. We're going to be here for a while."

Blitz pulled the massive hatches shut and turned the

heavy lockwheels to seal them, then moved to stand beside the wiry ringleader. Cale heard a noise behind him. Wincing, he turned to see the rest of the gang members climbing up out of a hatch in the floor.

Along with Klegg and his lieutenants, they formed a circle around Cale and began to close in.

– 16 –

Klegg stepped back from the fray, not willing to wrinkle his new shirt or smear it with blood or sweat. Inside the sealed headquarters chamber, the rest of his gang members held a struggling Cale—eight against one, this time.

Probably not the finest examples of the Human race, Tek would have said. So far, Cale hadn't seen much to recommend New Marrakech or the Drifters, or Humans in general.

Klegg's lips spread into a broad, awful smile on his narrow face. Taunting, he touched the ring that dangled on a chain around his neck. Sam Tucker's ring.

Cale tried to maintain his dignity. Even in his position, overpowered by the gang members, he struck at the ringleader's weak spot. "Gee, Klegg, what are you going to do now that you don't have a little alien girl to stuff in an airlock?"

Cale spat at Blitz, who was twisting his arm behind

his back. The bull-necked bully scowled in disgust and butted his thick skull against Cale's head, making his ears ring.

The other gang members laughed, while Cale tried to shake off the dizziness. He concentrated on Klegg instead. "Look at all these big oafs against one kid. It's actually sort of flattering. You must really be afraid of me, Klegg. What are you going to do for an encore to make yourself feel big and tough?"

The ringleader tapped a finger on his lips as if deep in thought. "Maybe we'll feed you into a food recycler with the other squirtles and shaft-rats. That would benefit the whole community."

"You might as well dump yourself in with the rest of the garbage," Cale said. "That would benefit the community even more."

"Ooooh, I'm hurt," Klegg said.

Cale looked past the sweaty, smelly bodies of the crowding bullies to scan the chamber. Klegg's gang had refitted the reactor core and cleaned it up to make it their headquarters, but they had not done a thorough job. Rust spots and water stains marred the metal surface and a strange purplish fungus crawled in patches up the curved, bolt-studded wall.

Interior lights flickered, and exposed wires dangled like black spiderwebs. An air-recycler groaned as its fan clanked against the drive belt. Globs of hardened food had clogged a broken nozzle with inedible extrusions and sealed a food-processing unit shut. A luxury massage cot—stolen, no doubt—was crammed into a corner, apparently no longer functional. Klegg's gang seemed as good at maintaining machinery as anyone else on New Marrakech.

The ringleader still seemed to be pondering the question of what to do with Cale, preferably something amusing . . . and painful.

Cale taunted him again. "Don't you find it ludicrous that you need *eight* goons to hold me down?" He jabbed with his elbow. All eight of the "goons" jabbed back.

Klegg ran his finger along the ring chain. "There's nothing more boring than a sore loser."

"You only got my ring because you grabbed a little girl and threw her in an airlock." Cale rolled his eyes. "Another demonstration of your bravery and power."

"Oh, shut him up, Blitz," Klegg said.

Cale surprised them all by bursting into laughter. "See what I mean, guys? He can't even shut me up by himself. He's got to have someone else do it for him. Does he have you wipe his mouth when he eats? Man, I'd be totally embarrassed to have Klegg as my fearless leader." He turned to the bull-necked thug. "He's better suited to cleaning lint from under your toenails, Blitz, than bossing you around."

A deep frown creased the bully's forehead. "I don't have lint in my toenails."

Now Klegg began to look disturbed. "Don't listen to the squirtle. He's trying to confuse you."

"Oh, now he thinks he can control what words penetrate the thick wax in your ears? Give me a break." Cale thrashed and turned his defiant glare on two of the other henchmen. "Think about it. You've got to be smarter than you look." The two thugs knitted their eyebrows, trying to decide if they had just been insulted.

"Klegg is a coward, too scared to fight me himself, one on one."

"I am not afraid," Klegg said, "and the rest of my gang knows it."

"When's the last time you demonstrated that you were fit to be a leader? Torturing little girls? Ganging up eight to one? Show them you're not afraid of me."

"Don't flatter yourself, squirtle," Klegg said. "Why should I waste my time showing off? There's nothing in it for me."

Cale seized the opportunity. "I'll make it worth your while. I've got something you need."

Klegg made a vile-sounding chuckle. "What can a shaft-rat like you possibly have that I would need?"

Cale jerked his chin to indicate the broken food-prep unit. "A bit of mechanical know-how, for starters. You guys couldn't fix a toothbrush."

"I don't use a toothbrush," said the bull-necked henchman.

Cale wrinkled his nose. "No surprise there." He turned back to Klegg, yanking his arms until one of the bullies let loose. "I want my ring back, and I'm willing to fight you for it. *You alone*, Klegg—not your army of brain-washed slaves."

The bullies bristled at that.

"Prove yourself a leader, Klegg. And if I trounce you into a stain just like that scum on the side wall there"— he jerked his head to indicate the purple fungus on the metal bulkhead—"then I get my ring back."

"It'll never happen," Klegg said.

"Then what's to worry about?" Cale replied, sounding reasonable. "If I lose, I fix all the equipment here in your

HQ. I can even install a video surveillance unit, screens and cameras, so that you could sit back, warm and comfy in your chairs, and keep watch on your whole section of New Marrakech."

"You could do that?" one of the bullies said.

"Klegg sure can't," Cale said.

The ringleader took an uncertain step backward, but his bully followers began to mutter to each other. "That sounds fair . . ." "I want to see Klegg fight . . ." "Be nice to have the food-prep unit working again. I'm tired of yeast cakes."

Cale jerked his other arm free now and took a step forward to glare at Klegg. He held out his hand, palm up. "Or would you rather just forfeit the fight and give me the ring right now?"

In answer, Klegg unbuttoned his rainbow-silk shirt and removed it in preparation for the contest.

Cale had never fought in zero-gravity before.

As soon as he saw the gang members split apart and make their way to chairs and hold-bars on the side wall of the reactor chamber, Cale noticed that the new furniture had been bolted down. Nothing seemed to be moveable. *Uh-oh*, he thought.

Klegg cracked his knuckles and stood in the middle of the floor. "You ready?"

Before Cale could answer, Blitz shut off the gravity generator.

"What in the—?" Cale stumbled backward and found that the recoil from his footsteps sent him drifting into the air. "Hey!" He thrashed his arms and legs, but found no purchase, no resistance.

Then the wiry ringleader launched himself off the floor, arms straight down at his sides to make himself a streamlined projectile. Klegg barreled at him like a missile and struck Cale in the gut, driving both of them into the nearest metal wall. Cale slammed hard, his breath knocked out of him.

When Klegg tried to bounce back with one foot, Cale reacted quickly enough to grab the bully's arms and swing him around, rotating about their common center of mass. Cale was amazed at the swiftness and smoothness of the movement.

Klegg banged his head against the metal, much harder than Cale had ever expected him to hit. The ringleader's shoulders struck a patch of purple fungus that left a misshapen violet smear on the plates and on his back.

"Okay, this is not a problem. I can do this," Cale muttered to himself. A subconscious part of his mind analyzed the zero-G conditions and told him what to do. Letting instinct take over, he kicked off from the wall and drifted into the center of the reactor chamber, slowly turning somersaults in the air.

He saw hold-bars at odd places around the room. Klegg and his gang probably practiced often with the gravity shut off. Perhaps the bullies captured street urchins in the souks and brought them in here to be tossed around, wailing children bounced like sport balls from one thug to another until they grew tired of the game and dumped the kids back out into the alleys.

Recovering himself, Klegg soared after Cale, an angry grimace on his lean face.

As Cale held on to a bar near the ceiling, he understood the trick: without gravity, neither of them could change his trajectory in mid-flight. Once he launched, he had to hit another object before he could alter course.

Cale waited at the wall while Klegg hurtled toward him, arms extended, ready to strangle his opponent. But an instant before the ringleader reached him, Cale launched himself sideways, flying easily away. The bully could only snarl at him as he flew past.

The other gang members howled and cheered and made unimaginative, insulting catcalls at both opponents.

Cale took off his left shoe, hoping to use it as a clumsy weapon. When Klegg turned his back and grabbed a hold-bar to reorient and launch himself again, Cale tossed the shoe with deadly accuracy. It spun like a whirligig in the air.

"Klegg, look out!" one of the bullies said.

He whirled to see what they were talking about, turning toward Cale just in time for the shoe to smack him full in the face. Klegg spluttered in outrage and grabbed for the shoe, but it ricocheted off his head and spun away in a different direction. A streak of red blood dribbled from the bully's smashed nose, broke into smaller droplets, and floated through the air.

"Ready to give up yet?" Cale said. "Or would you prefer to chase me around some more?"

Furious, Klegg worked at a set of concealed buttons by the joints of the hold-bar. The metal rod popped out of its couplings and left the ringleader holding a deadly club. "Okay, that's a lot worse than a shoe," Cale muttered.

Again, Klegg launched himself straight toward Cale, who drifted too slowly toward the wall. Cale tried to swim through the uncooperative air, but made no progress. Seeing no other way, he took off his right shoe and held it, heel outward, in a defensive posture.

Klegg's gang members hooted and howled. The rough audience grasped handles and settled themselves more comfortably in their support seats on the wall as they watched their leader fly toward Cale.

Klegg slashed with his ominous metal pipe like a baseball bat. Cale hung stranded like a balloon in the middle of the chamber. He could always duck and twist around so that the hard pipe would whistle past him. At the right moment, Cale kicked out, catching Klegg in the sternum, sending them both flying in opposite directions.

The ringleader hit, recoiled from the wall, and shot back toward him, still holding the deadly metal club. From an unexpected direction, Cale felt something cold and slimy splatter the back of his head. He touched his hair, then looked at his fingers, which dripped with bright, sticky red, though he felt no pain. With a lurch of dismay, he thought his skull had been split open— but then, from the giggling laughter, he realized that the bullies must have thrown rotten fruit at him.

Cale ignored them and watched Klegg come toward him. Another soft, bright tomato splattered his chest like a gunshot wound—before Klegg crashed into him, driving them both against the metal wall. Cale's ears rang from striking one of the heavy, round bolt-heads, and he wrenched himself to one side as Klegg swung with the pipe.

With a loud bang and a vibration of metal, the rod spanged off the hull of the reactor core. The recoil of the blow pushed Klegg backward, but he clutched Cale's shirt, pulling them both out into the middle of the air.

Still holding his shoe in his right hand, Cale smacked Klegg in the face again, causing the ringleader to let go and spit out blood that ran from his lip. Klegg swiped the pipe through the air again, but Cale was already drifting away, out of reach.

"I don't remember any rule saying we could use weapons," Cale said.

"Nobody said anything about rules *at all*." Klegg laughed. "When I fight, there are no rules. Easier to keep track of things that way."

As Cale drifted across the open area, Klegg came after him with a malicious grin, like a shark cruising toward its victim.

"Okay, not a problem," Cale said, watching the bully float toward him on a predictable course, unable to change or maneuver. "I can live with no rules."

He dug into his pocket and pulled out the bag of crumbled red pepper that the food stall proprietor had given him. He opened the bag and flung the contents out into the air. In the zero-gravity, the cloud of hot scarlet dust slowly, inexorably expanded right into Klegg's path.

The bully looked surprised, then suspicious. He thrashed but drifted into the cloud of pepper, unable to get out of the way no matter how he flapped his hands. His mouth and eyes opened wide, and he gasped, sucking in the powdered spice. Klegg coughed and sneezed, then squeezed his eyes shut and rubbed them until tears streamed down his cheeks.

At the opposite wall, Cale reached out to catch himself on a hold-bar. Hand over hand, he pulled himself down to the floor again while Klegg still choked and wailed in midair, completely helpless.

"I think that counts as a victory, wouldn't you say?" Cale looked at the bullies and raised his eyebrows.

Smug, Blitz flipped a switch on the gravity generator, and Klegg tumbled down, crashing onto the floor near one of the sealed hatches. All the bullies laughed.

The ringleader got to his hands and knees, red-faced, teary-eyed, and coughing. Klegg swayed to his feet and staggered blindly around looking for water, looking for the door.

"I'll take my father's ring back now," Cale said. "You've lost, Klegg."

Before he could reclaim his prize and mark his victory, one of Klegg's gang members burst through a hatch in the floor. "You gotta see this. There's a fleet of Drej ships—all around New Marrakech."

Without warning, the aliens began a full-scale attack. . . .

— 17 —

Nineteen identical Drej Stingers converged upon the isolated Drifter colony . . . and opened fire.

It was the largest group of alien fighters seen together in the ten years since the Drej had gone dormant after destroying Earth. But the pulsing energy aliens were now ready to cause more damage, to finish the job they had begun a decade before.

New Marrakech was an airtight cluster of vessels and refugee ships, converted to living spaces and compartmentalized for safety. The broad open areas were covered by plazdomes and atmosphere containment fields. The Stingers circled the ugly cluster of Human vessels and structures, seeking weak sections and primary points of attack.

The outer, most vulnerable containers were storage pods attached to the main hub. Drej blasters split open the seams as if making surgical incisions. Molten metal and freezing water gushed out to form sparkling comets in space. Food supplies scattered and floated away. And a few hapless victims Drifted in the cold vacuum like lost snowflakes.

More Drej weapons targeted a window-filled sphere that perched like a Christmas ornament atop the tallest protrusion. The observation dome was an expensive dwelling owned by one of the richest traders on New Marrakech. Now, Drej beams vaporized the windows, and decompression caused the sphere to explode. Only the rich trader's automatic defense systems saved the colonists who lived in the tower beneath him by sealing off the atmosphere with an emergency containment field.

Within moments, the Drej had destroyed a handful of easy targets. Then the nineteen Stingers clustered again, reassessed their attack plan, and struck at a new set of vulnerable targets.

As the first explosions rang like cannon fire through the Drifter colony, Klegg picked himself up off the floor. Battered and sore, bleeding from his nose and smashed lips, the bully watched the artificial lights flicker around him. His eyes and mouth still burned from the hot pepper dust. He could barely see.

Hearing the chaos of screams and alarms outside, his gang let out cries of confusion, and the glow of triumph faded on Cale Tucker's face.

Klegg forced himself not to rub his stinging eyes, to let the flow of tears wash away the spicy powder. He clutched the chain around his neck and stumbled toward the escape hatch before Cale could stop him. Under no circumstances did he intend to give the kid's ring back.

Another explosion rumbled through New Marrakech,

making the floorplates buck like waves beneath his feet. Already nauseated with vertigo from zero-gravity fighting, Klegg could barely figure out in which direction he needed to flee. But before his enemy could come at him again, he decided to disappear into the convoluted streets where he could vanish amidst the chaos. He intended to pick up the pieces later.

Klegg knew Blitz and his gang could take care of Cale easily enough . . . *if* they had an inclination to do so. His cheeks burned as much with shame and rage as his eyes did from the stinging pepper. Cale had humiliated Klegg in front of his own gang. Now the other bullies might be more inclined to laugh at their ringleader than help him.

The hatch opened, and Klegg stumbled through it. Recovering quickly, Cale shouted at the ringleader, but he couldn't get to the hatch fast enough. Klegg slammed the metal door in his face.

Slipping out into the walkway, Klegg wondered exactly what this ring meant. Was there more to it than he'd thought? When he'd taken it in exchange for the little alien girl's life, the ring had seemed only an interesting trinket, not particularly valuable. But why was Cale Tucker willing to sacrifice so much to get it back? What was it about this piece of junk?

Klegg wanted to find out. He raced out into the crowded, panicked streets of New Marrakech, ducking his head as the firebombing from space continued all around him.

Cale saw the beaten ringleader flee like a muddy pack-rodent back into its lair. "Hey, stop him!" he shouted after the door slammed, though he doubted anyone would listen. "I beat the guy in a fair fight. He owes me my ring back."

The rest of Klegg's gang, though, seemed more interested in the disaster and the thunderous explosions of the outside attack.

Cale planted his feet more firmly on the metal floor and grasped the wheel on the exit hatch Klegg had vanished through. The thick metal walls of the reactor chamber rang like a church bell struck with a sledgehammer, and the lights winked out. A muscular body collided with Cale, making him lose his grip on the hatch and fall backward. The bullies scrambled about like a hive of blinded bees. Climbing back to his feet, Cale was jostled and pushed in different directions. Just then the gravity generator failed, and he found himself sailing up into weightless darkness.

"Not the best time to lose weight," he groaned. He tried to figure out which direction he was flying, since the chamber was an intense, murky black around him. He'd been focused on racing toward the exit hatch, but he couldn't recall how close he was to the wall.

Cale tucked his head and his knees, making his body into a ball, dreading the moment when he would smash into the wall. Klegg's gang found themselves drifting about weightless and yelling for help. Two of the panicked bullies unintentionally punched him in the chin and kicked him in the back as they struggled in the air around him. Inside the sealed hideout, the drumbeat of explosions jarred loose pieces of equipment and personal possessions, which now tumbled about in the darkness, creating an obstacle course of unseen booby traps.

When one bully's broad shoulder bumped him, Cale pushed himself off of it and flew in a different direction until he collided with someone else's bony elbow. The frightened bully screamed, as if he were being attacked by aliens. Cale crashed into a floating metal box and cut his forearm. He pushed the object away, and he heard it smack into somebody's head with an accompanying outcry.

Cale had to get down, had to find the hatch again. Finally, he found the wall—by smashing into it with his face. Not exactly how he'd meant to orient himself, but good enough. Using sweaty palms, he frogwalked along the curved bulkhead until he snagged one of the holdbars and used it to pull himself down. His feet finally struck the floor—or was it the ceiling?—and he moved toward where he thought the exit hatch was.

When he did encounter the rounded arch, he grabbed the edges, operated the manual controls, turned the lock-wheel and shoved at the hatch, working against weightlessness as he tried to gain leverage. The door finally groaned open, flooding the darkened chamber with light.

Behind him eight bullies floated in the air, stranded like flies caught in an invisible web. But Cale didn't care about them right now—not that he ever had. He ducked through the hatch and staggered into the streets. Shaking sweat and blood out of his eyes, he blinked in astonishment at the flames and destruction erupting all around him.

After Iji had watched Klegg and his cowardly gang take Cale, she'd followed them without being seen, around corners, through dim alleys, to the rusty old reactor pod they had made into their headquarters.

While she waited, she hung back and smiled to herself. Maybe now that the bullies had taken him prisoner, Cale was counting on *her* to rescue *him*. Iji promised herself that she wouldn't let her pod-brother down. He would be so proud of her.

Unfortunately, when the chamber hatches sealed, she had no way of getting inside. This wasn't like a Vusstran house or factory, where she could always find a transparent patch of cermet to peek through. No, this was an empty engine reactor chamber, designed to contain explosive forces when a starship blasted into space.

Using her agility and gripping with her clawed fingers and toes, Iji climbed the plated side of the chamber looking for a way in. Overhead, the normally clear atmosphere fields shimmered like an aurora storm, and she wondered what could be going on out there. She reached the top of the armored vessel, but found no way to gain entrance, other than the hatches down below. She heard a bang inside, as if something hard had struck the wall.

Frowning, she was trying to think of another way to tackle the problem when she saw the blue streaks of Drej Stingers overhead. The alien attack ships fired upon the clustered Drifter vessels. Electrical discharges rippled like lightning across the broad atmosphere field.

Iji gasped. If the overhead containment failed, all of the air would gush out into space, taking objects, vehicles, supplies . . . and Iji herself.

She flattened her body against the top of the reactor chamber and wondered how she was going to get to safety. Or even where safety might be. And what could she do to help Cale?

She heard battering and pounding inside the chamber, but the bullies didn't sound like they were trying to get out. Maybe they hadn't even noticed the attack yet. Then, when the Stingers blasted open cargo containers in the outer storage ring, the whole Drifter colony lurched. Iji slid toward the opposite edge of the reactor chamber roof and nearly fell off. She swung herself over the edge and scrambled back down the curved side, trying to reach street level.

To her surprise, a hatch opened directly beneath her and a figure staggered out. Klegg! He looked roughed up, his hair disheveled, his face bloodied, his rainbow-silk shirt gone. He looked as if he'd been beaten up, and Iji hoped Cale had done it.

As new explosions pounded the underside of New Marrakech, Iji released her hold and let herself drop—directly onto Klegg. Her unexpected landing knocked Klegg flat onto the street.

The bully ringleader reacted like a sprung animal trap, jabbing both elbows into her. Then he bounced to his feet in utter terror. Instead of sneering as he had done when he stuffed her in the airlock, the bully backed away from her. "Leave me alone, brat! I can't deal with you right now."

Iji got up and looked for something to throw at him. "Come back here, you coward, and I'll knock you onto the street again." She hoped Klegg wouldn't turn around, because she didn't really know how she could fight him. But the ringleader fled instead as the Drej attack continued.

He raced toward the tall tower of a central spaceship, an old rocket vessel that had been converted into a shiny, high-tech mosque at the center of New Marrakech. Iji was tempted to race after him, but decided it was more important to go make certain Cale was all right.

Inside the *Sword Ring*, Tek sat in his pilot's seat and frantically worked the controls. He had noticed the Drej fleet's approach on his scanners and sounded an alarm—but in the end it had made no difference. Even fore-warned, the Humans had no defenses against the alien attack, no weapons at all that were a match for the Drej.

If only the Qu'utians had finished their research and developed a counterstrike ability . . .

Cale and Iji were both gone, lost in the streets of the Drifter colony. He knew how resourceful the two could be, yet in the face of such devastation, he didn't think they could survive without help.

But Tek did not know how he could reach them.

Even if they returned safely, Tek couldn't get the *Sword Ring*'s engines started without the vital thrust flux stabilizer. The TR-Epsilon Z had been severely damaged the last time they had encountered the Drej.

He powered his engines, trying to get an ignition spark. Half of the lights on his panel winked green—an improvement—but the other half remained red. This ship wasn't going anywhere.

The Drej attack continued. He watched the Stingers on his screens as they orbited around the Drifter colony like a pack of voracious glarns, tearing and shredding the defenseless Human habitat.

Mohammed Bourain had given him a condensed data

archive, the remaining clues he needed to finish his ecological restoration work based on Sam Tucker's research. If Tek could just get home to Vusstra, he could use these techniques to create a new spark of life on his crumbling world.

If he could get away from here.

Mohammed had been happy to share, knowing that Sam Tucker would have wanted his research used for the benefit of all peaceful races. As the energy explosions continued to rain on New Marrakech, Tek hoped Mohammed was all right. The merciless Drej assault destroyed structures indiscriminately. Tek knew how ruthless the alien combat forces could be, but he couldn't understand why they still needed to pound the surviving Humans to their knees. He hoped the aliens were not bent on the complete destruction of the colony.

Did they mean to make all of the Human race extinct? Why had they chosen to attack New Marrakech? And why now?

Tek felt cold dread inside as he remembered how his own ship had been chased through the Qu'utian asteroid field. Cale had destroyed a lone Stinger here, outside the Drifter colony.

Perhaps they themselves had led the Drej to New Marrakech. And now all of the colonists would pay for that mistake.

—18—

Cale stumbled out of the crazy fun house of Klegg's hideout, blinded by the colony's artificial sunlight and clumsy from the sudden return to gravity. Disoriented, he had just steadied himself against a curved metal wall, when a huge explosion nearly knocked him off his feet again.

The last thing he expected to see was Iji charging toward him. "Cale! There you are."

Before he could say a word, she leaped on him and gave him a big hug. He swayed but somehow kept himself from falling over backward. Unwilling to admit that he was glad to see his pod-sister, Cale groaned.

She touched the smear of blood on his forehead. "You're hurt!"

"Really? Kind of you to notice." Fuming, his mind still on the ring, he looked in vain down the narrow, crooked streets for any sign of the bully leader. Cale had won the challenge, beaten the bully at his own game, and Klegg had still run away with Sam Tucker's ring.

With a resounding detonation, a geyser of coolant gas burst from a pipe beneath the metal streets of New Marrakech. Overhead, through the atmosphere fields, he could see the deadly blue Stingers cruising around the Drifter colony, firing at random. Cale's ears popped as a distant boom of decompression swept through the cluster. With a clang of heavy, automatic doors, a small domed section sealed itself off to protect the rest of the space city.

He didn't want to give up his search for Klegg, but realized it was too late now. Frantic people ran through the streets, robes torn and flapping. Panic had set in as the crowds scrambled for shelter.

He grabbed Iji's scrawny arm. "Come on, Ijit. We have to find Tek. Maybe we can get out of here."

"The ship doesn't have a thrust flux stabilizer yet!" Iji said. "And you don't have your ring."

"Forget the ring," Cale said. "We're in danger out here."

Iji planted her broad feet on the ground and dragged her heels. "But I saw where Klegg went. I know where you can find him. Don't give up when you're so close!"

Now Cale hesitated. *Victory through persistence*. He touched the tattoo on his arm. He had come so far to get his father's ring back.

Iji tugged his arm. "Come on!"

"All right," Cale said. He'd won the challenge—and now he meant to claim his prize. "Where is he?"

She pointed toward the tall minaret of the old-style rocketship that served as New Marrakech's main mosque. "In there."

"Funny," Cale said. "He didn't seem like much of a religious sort to me."

"I think he just wanted to get out of sight as fast as he could."

Cale strode through the smoke, determined now, and Iji scurried after him. They pushed past crowds of people in loose and colorful djellabas, women in brilliant silk gowns, men with white caps and bright, terrified eyes. Cale couldn't believe Iji had managed to track the fleeing bully through such a frenzy. "I always thought you were just a sneak and a tattletale, Ijit. But you did good this time."

The Vusstran girl beamed, bobbing her head and smiling hugely. "I know how much that ring means to you."

They made their way to the entrance arch of the mosque. Refugees flooded through the streets, seeking sanctuary. Some rushed to the safety of the streamlined silvery structure, while others helped the injured or put out spreading fires.

The interior of the old spaceship had been converted into a beautiful place of worship. After fleeing the destruction of Earth and arriving at this rendezvous point, the vessel was gutted, dismantled, and redecorated— never to fly again. But the shell had become a monument to the best and most exotic parts of Human culture. From the ashes of Earth, the people here had created something wondrous.

Inside what had once been a primary cargo bay stood five beautiful fountains for the faithful to use in the ritual washing of hands and feet before beginning their prayers. Old water pumps and pipes spilled water into basins inlaid with plaz-tile and metal chips, making the fountains works of art rather than simple plumbing fixtures. Per ancient tradition, men and women prayed separately in the mosque, but now the terrified refugees mixed together inside the spaceship.

Cale raked his eyes across the crowd, trying to find the bully ringleader. He narrowed his green eyes, trying to adjust to the slanted light that came through kleersteel portholes converted into beautiful windows. At the far end of the cargo bay, a mihrab arch stood on a rotating platform that pivoted with the time of day, so that it faced the approximate position of where Mecca would have been on old Earth.

A robed and bearded old man led the people in prayers as explosions from the attack continued outside. All along the walls, smooth metal plates were adorned with the beautiful scrollwork of Arabic calligraphy, handwritten verses from the Koran.

Iji spotted the bully first. Klegg was hunched behind the farthest of the five fountains, splashing water on his bruises and injuries, washing the blood from his face— obviously believing he'd gotten away.

But as soon as he saw Iji and Cale at the entrance to the mosque, Klegg's swollen eyes flew wide open. With bare feet, he sprinted across the floor into the women's area, elbowing terrified worshippers aside. Cale broke into a run with Iji racing after him.

The prayer leader stopped in mid-sentence. Begging forgiveness for the disruption, Cale dodged people kneeling in prayer, trying not to jostle them. But when he tripped over a striped gray djellaba, Cale sprawled across the deck, skinning his palms and his arms. He managed to scramble to his feet again just as he saw

Klegg open a small hatch that led behind the walls of the cargo hold, beyond the mosque's worship center and into the once-functional bowels of the derelict spaceship.

Klegg swung the hatch shut and scampered into the darkness, but Cale shoved the metal door open with his shoulder. He and Iji pushed their way into shadows that smelled of dust, oil, and grease. Cale didn't know where he was going, and the tunnels looked dark and ominous. Almost certainly a trap.

But he didn't dare give up now.

Outside, a handful of still-functional Drifter ships broke free of the moorings where they had attached themselves. Crammed full of as many refugees as they could hold, the scattered vessels pulled away from the main hub of New Marrakech and struggled to gain distance . . . hoping the Drej wouldn't waste time targeting them.

Two small craft, flown by foolhardy pilots, powered up outdated weapons systems and zoomed toward the Drej fleet. Although it was a suicide mission, the pilots nevertheless fired their forward blasters. Barely able to aim with their weapons computers, they hoped they would hit something.

The Stingers swirled into a defensive formation and blew the first of the two vessels into a cloud of sparkling debris. The second pilot flew erratically, either with sophisticated evasive maneuvers, or just uncertain navigational control. He fired three times before his weapons systems gave out; then, with no hope and no defenses, he crashed into the nearest Drej ship. Both exploded into spangles of light.

All of the Human fighters had been destroyed, and eighteen Drej Stingers remained.

Cale would have been completely lost in the stuffy confines behind the walls of the mosque if the original vessel had not so closely resembled Tek's old-model TR-Epsilon Z. Iji's Vusstran eyes seemed adequate for seeing in the dark, and the faint flickers of emergency lights with long-dimmed batteries gave her enough illumination so that she could direct him.

"There, Cale. A ladder ahead." She stopped to listen; Cale could hear running footsteps: Klegg's bare feet. "We'd better hurry if we're going to catch him." Iji ran forward, calling, "Watch out for that corner!" half a second after he had already smashed into it. Cale followed her more carefully until his eyes adjusted to the gloom. He found the rungs of a crew ladder, and cocked his head to listen.

The mosque chambers comprised what had been the ship's large cargo bays. The pinnacle of the rocket, once filled with guidance and control systems, now served as a high balcony from which the muezzins sang out their call to prayer several times each day.

But Klegg had gone *down*, descending to the engineering deck and the thruster control chambers of the long-dead spacecraft.

Iji scrambled down the crew ladder first, moving with the speed and agility of a gecko. Cale hurried after her, one sore hand on a rung while the other one lowered him down. His knuckles were skinned from the fight and still seeping blood.

The shadows were thicker in the abandoned engine

compartment. Iji hurried ahead, listening to Klegg lumber about, trying to hide. Afraid to show himself, the bully did not turn on a handlight that would call attention to his position.

The long-dormant engines smelled of dust and oil. They had been shut down for a full decade since this spacecraft had docked at what would become New Marrakech. Old boxes, clothes, and spare parts were stacked inside cold drive-reactor chambers that would never be used again.

Above, through the thick metal ceiling, Cale could hear the chanting prayers, the desperate movement of people. Klegg had led them directly under the cargo chamber that served as a prayer room. Piping ran like a shadowy network of blood vessels across the ceiling overhead; Cale decided they must be beneath the fountains, near the water-storage cisterns. The floor beneath him was damp.

Iji scuttled along with slippery footsteps, a whisper of noise. On the other side of the dim engine chambers, Cale could hear the bully's hiss of pain as he stubbed a toe, and then a clang as he knocked over some spare piping.

Like an ominous thunderstorm, muffled Drej explosions reverberated through the spaceship hull and through the deck underfoot.

"Wait," Iji said. Cale was surprised to hear her voice so far across the room. "I think I've found the bypass—"

Suddenly, emergency lights came on in the engine compartment. The batteries were mostly dead, with barely enough juice to squeeze a dull orange flicker from the bulbs rather than gleaming scarlet light. But after the blindingly dark shadows, even this amount of illumination was enough to seem bright as day.

Seeing no place to hide among the giant generators and piping and storage boxes, Klegg bolted out from the shadows that no longer concealed him. "Leave me alone! Can't you see this colony is under attack?"

"Give me my ring back." Cale strode forward. "Save yourself a lot of trouble."

The bully looked hunted now, his shadowed eyes flicking from side to side. "Where are your priorities?" he asked, sounding like a whiny child.

"My priority is to get my ring back," Cale said, his voice hard and unyielding. "My father gave it to me."

Iji scrambled out away from the lighting controls. Even Cale's little Vusstran pod-sister looked menacing to Klegg. Instead of surrendering, though, the defeated ringleader spotted another metal ladder hanging halfway down from the ceiling. Making a desperate jump, he caught the bottom rung, and hauled himself hand over hand toward a hatch in the ceiling. He didn't even take time to laugh.

"Hey, come back!" Cale shouted.

"You don't want to go up there," Iji called, looking up at the ceiling piping. But Klegg put on a burst of speed and reached the round hatch screw that held the metal lid in place, closing access to a ceiling compartment.

Iji raced over to Cale and pushed him back out of the way. "I guarantee you, he doesn't want to do that."

Klegg turned the access wheel. He looked down with a final glare of triumph as he gave the wheel another turn, ready to pull down the hatch and climb up through the ceiling deck to freedom.

Now Cale noticed what Iji had seen: it wasn't exactly the ceiling Klegg was attempting to enter, but a tank of some sort. Then he remembered they were directly under the fountains and water cisterns that fed into the plumbing systems.

Klegg yanked the overhead hatch open—and a sudden, gushing waterfall hammered him off the ladder. Thousands of liters roared down, pummeling him like a dozen firehoses.

The bully thrashed on the floor, spitting and sputtering like a fish tossed out of a net, but the pouring water pinned him down while the cistern drained. Runoff flowed across the engine room deck toward drains in the floor.

Since he had lost both of his shoes in the zero-gravity duel, Cale's bare feet were soaked up to his ankles. But he didn't mind. Water from the cistern continued to trickle and flow until the last drops emptied out of the mouth of the open hatch.

Klegg lay gasping on the floor and finally got to his hands and knees, drenched and bedraggled. He looked like the mud-covered packrodent Cale had fought in the bubbling mudpots on Vusstra.

Before the bully could get his wits about him again, Cale sloshed through the puddles and bent over to grab the ring on the chain around Klegg's neck. "I'll take this now, thank you." He snapped it off. Klegg winced as the chain broke, and Cale made a great show of placing his father's ring back onto the middle finger of his left hand.

"What's the big deal about that ring?" the bully demanded, then coughed water, still blinking his reddened eyes. "Is it worth a lot? Does it do something special?"

"I have no idea," Cale answered, admiring the way the gold circlet gleamed below his skinned knuckles. "But you'll never find out."

He looked over at Iji, expecting to see her clap her hands with glee at how he had beaten the ringleader— or at least laugh about how Klegg had humiliated himself in his efforts to escape. Instead, she was intent on something inside one of the mosque's old engine compartments. She tinkered at one of the open access grates that led into the stabilizers of the dormant reactors.

Cale felt as if he couldn't lose now, and Klegg didn't worry him at all. Even so, with the attack going on outside, he didn't want to stay any longer than was necessary. "C'mon, Ijit. Let's get going."

Iji turned to him, her saucer eyes wide, her lips curled in another broad smile. "Wait, Cale! Come see what I found."

-19-

Cale and Iji raced back into the smoky, chaos-filled streets of New Marrakech, feeling exhilarated and victorious for a change. They left the rocketship mosque behind, but because the tall minaret tower was symmetrical, they couldn't be sure which direction they were heading.

"We've got to get back to the *Sword Ring*," Iji said, clutching her package tightly.

"Gee, figured that out all by yourself, huh?" Cale put his hands on his hips and tossed his grime-streaked blond hair out of his eyes. He looked one direction, then another, wishing he hadn't discarded the hand-drawn map the sandal maker had given him. "Did you also figure out which way we need to go?"

Iji said, "I've been following *you* all day."

With dismay, Cale viewed the burning buildings, collapsed structures, sections of New Marrakech closed off to prevent a decompression chain reaction. Everything seemed to have changed—except for the Stingers, still overhead, still firing. "A map wouldn't do us much good right now, anyway."

He had hated the dreary monotony of life on Vusstra, the muddy valleys and smoggy skies, the industrial facilities and abandoned factories. He'd complained that nothing ever happened there. But Cale couldn't say he liked this situation any better.

The souks were in flames. People abandoned their shops, racing toward evacuation ships. He could see through the shimmering atmosphere field that many docked vessels had already broken away, flying off into space in hopes that the Drej would not follow and pick them all off.

Cale did not doubt for a moment that the aliens could destroy New Marrakech if they wanted to. But who could know what the Drej wanted or what they might be thinking?

Overhead, a large orbiting hospital ship had arrived from the nearby planet of Solbrecht, a self-contained medical facility with armored walls and bright red markings (not that Cale believed the shimmering blue aliens would recognize or honor those markings).

A flurry of small craft continued to take off from the New Marrakech docking hub, flying into deep space or ferrying injured people up to the hospital facility. But the Solbrecht medical ship stood off at a relatively safe distance, while ambulance craft dodged the Drej to carry needy patients to the clinic in space.

The energy aliens shot halfheartedly at random ships, but mostly ignored them. The Drej goal seemed to be to divide the Earth survivors into smaller and more pathetic groups, to dim the flame of the Human spirit with each new blow. They were succeeding quite well.

Cale wondered how the brave Qu'utians would have responded to this overt attack. He glanced down at the Qu'utchaa symbol on his arm, remembering how that other race had watched the Drej attack their surface cities while they hid beneath, playing dead. But the Human colonists had no such option; they were sitting ducks in space, and the Drej had declared open hunting season.

Some escaping ships evacuated colonists and whatever supplies they'd had time to load. A few refugees stayed too long gathering keepsakes and possessions, things they had taken from old Earth. Unfortunately, their nostalgia caused them to miss their transport off of New Marrakech. They remained stranded on the colony as more buildings exploded.

"I think the spaceport area is over there," Iji said, tracing the launch trails of the ships they could see.

Whenever possible, they stopped someone and asked directions. Many of the people met Cale and Iji's questions with wild uncomprehending eyes, not daring to spare a moment or a breath to help. Finally, someone gestured down an alley, and the two ran along until they accosted another person for directions. This method seemed to work, getting them closer to the docking ports each time.

Cale and Iji had just come to a dead end in a twisted alleyway when they saw an old man sitting on a leather sling-chair in front of his darkened shop, just watching the Drej bombardment and refusing to move. He had sacrificed any seat he might have had on an escape ship just to remain at his home. "I said they'd be back someday, you know. Back to finish the job they started ten years ago," he said in a fatalistic tone, as if continuing a conversation that had begun before Cale and Iji had arrived. The old man calmly listened to their question, and gave them detailed instructions to the dock where they could find the TR-Epsilon Z.

Cale hoped by now that Tek had done what he could to prep the *Sword Ring* for immediate takeoff. If so, there might be just enough time to install the missing part. Cale didn't want to be stranded here. Iji clutched the precious bundle close to her chest as she scuttled along.

True to the resigned old man's descriptions, they found the docking port and the connecting tube that led to the classic ship that Tek had flown through the asteroid field of Qu'ut Prime, and then to New Marrakech.

They cycled through the ship's connecting tube and airlock, then raced up the access ramp. In the lower engine bay, frantic and distraught, Tek crouched with his head inside an open engine compartment, repositioning components and wires, but his wide eyes were forlorn and at a loss. For hours he had been trying to work around the damaged stabilizer module and devise a temporary solution for the *Sword Ring*. But he didn't have the necessary pieces.

When he saw Cale and Iji, he stood up so quickly he bumped his head on an access panel, winced, and then grinned with delight. "I was so worried. We're under attack."

Cale could barely keep himself from laughing. "Yeah, we kinda noticed. We need to get out of here, Tek."

"But the ship won't work." The Vusstran scientist

waved one hand at the engine's open access panels.

"Sure it will," Cale said, grinning with secret knowledge. "This is not a problem. I can fix this."

"I wish you'd come back hours ago." Tek picked up
a burnt-out component in disgust. "I studied the manuals
to figure out what to do, but . . ." He spread his hands
in a helpless gesture.

"Sorry I wasn't here, but I had some important business to complete." Cale lifted his hand to the light and
flashed the gold ring. "I've got what we came for."

Tek gasped. "So you persuaded that bully to give your
father's ring back, after all?"

"Well . . . he needed a little bit of convincing," Cale
said.

"And I helped convince him," Iji piped up.

When Tek cast his pod-daughter a doubtful look, Cale
said, "Yeah, the little Ijit proved herself useful for a
change."

Iji withdrew the bundle that she held close to her chest
and opened it up to reveal a greasy, bolt-studded gadget
that bristled with electrical leads, bent piping, and con-
duits; gleams of bright, silvery metal shone through the
patches of grime and rust. "We found a thrust flux stabilizer. It's an old model, not quite the same, but Cale
can adapt it for our ship."

"Uh-huh. You bet—I'm on it." Cale sounded skepti-
cal, but his heart swelled with pleasure and triumph
since he knew it was no longer an impossible challenge.

"I searched all over New Marrakech for one of those,"
Tek exclaimed. "Where did you find it?"

"In the spaceship mosque," Iji said. "It's an old vessel,

shut down and converted into a religious monument. Most of the vital components had already been stripped out, but a thrust flux stabilizer isn't something you need every day."

"Well, we need one *today*." Cale took the component from her clawed hands and nudged Tek. "I think I can handle it now. No time to waste. All I need are a few tools and a few seconds—then we can get out of here."

"I'll get the tools you need," Iji said. "Just name an instrument, and I'll pick it up for you."

"You'll be in the way, Ijit," Cale said.

"Since *when* have I ever been in the way?"

Cale was about to list the numerous times, but stopped and smiled. "All right. I could use a hand. Even one of yours." He gestured with his chin toward Tek. "Better get to the cockpit and be ready to launch as soon as the green lights come on."

Tek scrambled up the *Sword Ring*'s ladder, while Iji handed Cale delicate instruments as he asked for them. Cale looked at the systems that Tek had dismantled, picking up one component after another, testing them with sparking meters. A few pieces he discarded out-of-hand.

"Didn't need that anyway." The component clanked and rolled across the floor. "Didn't need that." *Thunk*. "And I certainly don't need to play music chips for the next few days." He tossed a circuit board over his shoulder, and it clattered against the wall.

Next, he picked up the mismatched thrust flux stabilizer and turned it clockwise and counter-clockwise, trying to find a way that all the connections could line up inside the TR-Epsilon Z. As close as he could make it, he jammed the piece in, bent the connectors one direction and another. A spark jumped from the panel and zapped his fingers, knocking him backward for a second, but Cale simply hissed at it, kept his comments to himself, and bent back to reconnecting the remaining systems.

He closed several secondary panels and powered up one subsystem after another. Finally, as the chain of circuits survived each new installation, Cale hooked up the primary component he and Iji had taken from the spaceship mosque. Holding his breath and closing his eyes, he snapped the final linkages together.

All the lights on the indicator board went red, then winked out.

He slammed his elbow down on the engine housing. "Come on!" The red lights flickered back to life, and then turned green.

Iji ran to the ladder and shouted up to Tek in the cockpit, "He's done! The engines are ready. Let's go!"

Cale and Iji raced each other to the top deck—just as they had so often raced each other to the astrascope at home—scrambling up the ladder to get to their seats.

Behind and below them, the survivors of New Marrakech continued to flee. People charged through the streets, searching for any way off the doomed colony. Most of the Drifter vessels had already flown away to safety, leaving the last few desperate people to find any remaining transport.

"All docking systems disengaged," Cale said as he threw himself into the seat beside Tek.

As soon as the engines lit up, people on the streets below began to rush toward their vessel. They pounded on the airlock hatch that led to the docking walkway. "Uh, we're going to have a mob on our hands if we don't get out of here soon," Cale said. "And if we bring any passengers on board, I don't think that thrust flux stabilizer will hold."

Iji peered out the window. "They're trying to crack open the connector tube."

The *Sword Ring*'s engines roared louder, pushing the vessel away from the dock.

"If they break that containment barrier, all the atmosphere will spill out," Iji said. "Why are they—"

"Frightened people don't always think of consequences, Iji," Tek answered, then punched the full-launch button.

The TR-Epsilon Z's engines blazed, sputtered, then flamed hot and strong. The thrust flux stabilizer took hold and settled in to its new job. Tek's ship pulled away from New Marrakech, but unlike the other Drifter vessels that swirled around aimlessly, unsure of where to go, Tek already had a course in mind.

As they pulled away from the glowing wreckage of the floating city, Cale saw to his surprise that the remaining Drej Stingers had withdrawn. The Stingers circled New Marrakech one more time, while the tiny refugee vessels floated away like chaff, many heading toward the Solbrecht hospital ship. Then, apparently considering their job finished, the Drej ships streaked off, quickly dwindling to pinpoints as they headed back toward their monstrous Mothership, far away in space.

Tek initiated the flight protocols and aimed the *Sword Ring* in another direction entirely. Together they sped away from New Marrakech, leaving the wounded Drifter colony behind.

—20—

After the devastation of New Marrakech, the return trip to Vusstra was as quiet as it was uneventful—to their great relief. They each spent some time in private thought. Once the three travelers reached home, however, all such quiet contemplation came to an end. Now that Tek had obtained the last pieces of information he'd needed about the Titan research, their real work could begin.

"Your father's legacy will save our world," Tek said to Cale.

Though his heart was full of hope, Cale put on an aloof expression, out of habit. "Well, I'd wait to see if it works first."

"That's what we're *here* for," Iji said, punching her pod-brother on one arm as if he was being inexcusably thickheaded.

They stood together out in the enclosed, desolate valley bounded by cracked, mined-out mountains and aban-

doned industrial equipment. The sun flickered through a
gray-brown haze of smog vapors, heating the air and
making it stink. Sulfurous fumes from the mudpots did
their best to overpower the pollution stench.

Three heavy XR400 dispersal ships cruised low across
the enclosed valley, scratching white exhaust trails on
the sky. Tek looked up at the craft, which he'd obtained
from his connections with the Vusstran military. "They
are marking the test grid over the valley," he said.
"Seven kecks long and four-point-three kecks wide, well
contained by the surrounding hills."

The sight of the test vessels brought the reality home
to Cale and he felt a tingle of excitement. Perhaps his
time away had allowed him to see this world through
fresh eyes and understand Tek's passion and hope.
"We'd better get up to the observation bunker."

Since receiving the data he'd needed from Mohammed Bourain on the Drifter colony, Tek had a fire within
him that Cale had never seen before. "Of course!" they
had heard Tek mutter over and over as he laid out var-
ious procedures. "Why didn't I remember that before?
Can you see the beauty of it?" Their home workshop
fairly boiled with enthusiastic activity. The Vusstran scientist had labored nonstop for weeks preparing a test run
of the plan that could, step by step, rejuvenate his home
planet.

Cale was reminded of the Qu'utian underground city
and their secret dreams. Previously, he would have considered the Vusstran Renewal Project an impossible
folly, but not anymore. He had seen what determination
could accomplish. Vusstrans were devoted and hard-

working, just as the Qu'utians were optimistic, persistent, determined, and resourceful.

But even after his recent travels, Cale still found little to admire in his fellow Humans, who had been conquered and defeated by the Drej—physically *and* mentally. Klegg and his cowardly, bullying lieutenants had lied to Cale, threatened to harm Iji, beaten Cale up, and stolen from him. None of the colonists on New Marrakech had been capable of simple maintenance or repairs. Even Sam Tucker, though supposedly brilliant, had abandoned him.

Cale still vividly remembered the old man sitting in his leather sling-chair during the attack on New Marrakech. He had surrendered completely, decided to sit back and watch everything die all around him, not even bothering to fight or flee. To Cale, the remnants of the Human race seemed like that.

Thus far, Cale had met no Humans deserving of his respect or trust. He didn't even feel *safe* among them. Tek's dream that the young man would find solidarity with fellow Human beings was still a long way off....

They took a skimmer that quickly brought them up the hillside to the old ore-processing site they had turned into their base camp. Vusstran scientists, assistants, workers, and government officials moved about, eager to see the results of the test. The magnitude of even this small project, as well as the continuing efforts across Vusstra, had required Tek to enlist the aid of numerous important people. But they deferred to him, knowing that this was his show.

"Ryt would have been so proud to see this," Tek said, his eyes moist with emotion as he remembered his wife's dreams. "All our work, the problem she died trying to solve . . ." He seemed to be in a daze. Cale and Iji stood closer.

Down in the blistered, barren valley, automated bio-generators puttered about, crawling over rocks, planting samples from the DNA library Tek had so assiduously collected. Energy-focusing towers crackled as they drew power from immense storage batteries and solar collectors. Tap-conduits had been drilled deep underground to the thermal areas that heated the mudpots, drawing more energy from the planet itself.

Cale looked at his wrist chronometer. "Only a few more minutes." From a podium in the middle of the base camp, a Vusstran politician gave a supposedly uplifting speech that nobody wanted to hear.

Working with Cale and Iji, Tek and his group of assistants had spent days breaking the ambitious plan into manageable stages. Tek recruited dozens of scientists he and Ryt had known; though overworked, he was definitely in his element.

"Hmm, yes. The basic components are all there," Tek had said. "We have all the resources, if we can just chemically rearrange them, recycle them into viable material again. Those substances don't have to be pollution—they can be the building blocks of life."

Inspecting the high-tech equipment assembled for the test project, Cale took his assigned tasks as seriously as he had anything in his life. "This will work. We can do this," he said, looking over a piece of apparatus a scientist had just brought him for review. "Now, what if we take this one step further? What if we link this imager to the topo-scanner? That way, we could get real-time feedback during the test and make adjustments from the central control board if we need to. Then, if everything works like it's supposed to . . ." He spread his hands and looked at the scientist.

"We could increase our yield by twenty percent. Yes, I'll have it done for you by morning." The Vusstran had nodded vigorously and rushed off.

After working round the clock for days, everything was ready. Cale and Iji stood next to each other at base camp, looking into the sky as the big XR400 dispersal craft came back in for a final calibration pass. Cale admired the skill of the seriously well-trained space jockeys at the helm.

"They'll do it in a single run," Iji said. "Much more efficient than a dozen separate hoversprayers." She sounded smug, and Cale knew the modification had been her suggestion, to maximize the effectiveness of the converter solution distribution process.

"Yes, Ijit. I hope they give you a medal."

The politician insisted that Tek come forward and make a speech. The Vusstran scientist, uncomfortable with the attention and uninterested in the distraction, stepped up to the voice projector and said, "Hmm, yes. Very well. Let the test begin."

The XR400 pilots had been waiting for the command, and now the dispersal ships flew over the ground, dumping sprays of the catalyst liquids. Inside the low, hastily erected observation bunkers, Vusstran technicians used Cale's imager and topo-scanner to monitor the progress and make adjustments from afar.

Generator towers crackled, focusing power through the Titan apparatus that Tek had built using plans developed with Sam Tucker. Finished with their dispersal run, while the clock ticked down to completion, the XR400 space jockeys roared back to the safety zone just as the boiling energy from the project reached its crescendo.

Cale said, "Better cover your—" just as a blaze of white and green and blue light washed over the valley like a flood, a spark of life like a firestorm. "Eyes," he finished in an awe-filled voice.

Energy crackled across the gasping, polluted ground, a wake up call for the dormant life within Vusstra. Thousands of biosamples surged to life, rejuvenated, regenerated. Organic chemicals, pollutants, waste material in the ground—rearranged like the pieces of a living puzzle—tumbled into new patterns, using genetic and geological information Tek had carefully catalogued and stored. Just waiting for this day.

The unbearable blaze of light across the valley below gradually dimmed, turned greener, finally fading to reveal a beautiful sight, an awesome landscape that was sharper than a memory and more vivid than a dream. Cale blinked, barely able to believe his eyes.

A clear stream rushed through the center of the valley where only a dry arroyo had been the day before. Fresh springs bubbled up from the ground, saturating the new meadow. Bright blossoms exploded from the angled thornbushes. Strange creatures, awakened from their storage tubes, took breaths of air that was sweeter than anything Vusstra had seen in centuries. Tucked into a basin at the elbow of the rugged mountains, a deep lake shimmered indigo blue; in the shallows strange creatures frolicked with the delight of being alive. Cale thought he recognized the *Meloplasmapod triorganus* that he had originally seen in Tek's lab.

Down by the former mudpots, a confused-looking packrodent waddled out of its den and blinked at the clear pools and lush, delicious vegetation. The bitter sulfur smell had been replaced with the scent of dew, grass, and flowers. The packrodent scuttled back inside its tunnel.

"Come on, let's go down there!" Iji cried. She and Cale grabbed Tek's arms and hauled him to the skimmers, while the rest of the gathered Vusstrans also rushed to see what they had created.

After the party that evening, during which scientists and politicians had promised funding for further stages in the Vusstran Renewal Project, Tek, Cale, and Iji gathered for a quiet family celebration. They snuggled into their lounge-nests in front of the cermet hearth in the library.

"To success and hope," Tek said, toasting with a glass of delicate moss-green algae distillate, a flavorful beverage reserved for special occasions.

Iji sat back, clearly contemplating the imminent changes in her life that would result from her entering group school. "I know my worries don't seem like much after today, now that it looks like Vusstra might be reawakened. But working on the test for the Renewal Project, I learned how good it felt to be part of a group. So I think I'm ready for group school now."

Tek smiled at her with pride. "And Cale must continue his group learning, too. He needs to be among Humans."

"Hey, don't expect me to go back to any Drifter colonies," Cale objected.

"But then you won't be here to visit me during school holidays," Iji said in a small, sad voice.

"Of course we will. We'll come back to visit you," Tek assured her.

"Besides," Cale said, "no matter where we are, Tek still has to supervise the Renewal Project, so we'll be back for lots of visits from wherever we are. And I assure you," he added in a dark voice, "it's not going to be a Drifter colony."

"To solidarity and working together to get things done," Iji added, lifting her glass. She glanced meaningfully at the tattoo on Cale's upper arm.

Studying the ring that was back in place on the middle finger of his left hand, Cale made the last toast. "To victory through persistence."

They all drank.

—21—

N ow that the Vusstran Renewal Project had begun to
expand to encompass larger portions of the polluted
continents, Tek knew it was time for Iji to go off to her
long-delayed group school.

Vusstran politicians and interviewers and ecstatic cit-
izens pestered him night and day. Tek had thought the
hard part of this project was finding the missing pieces
of Sam Tucker's research. But now he realized that had
merely been the beginning, and he saw no end in sight.

"I'm a scientist," he said, bemoaning his situation. He
and Cale were in Iji's room helping to pack her things
for the move to group school. "I worked in a very small
group with Sam Tucker on Earth. Ryt and I followed
our own research, and now that it's all proven to be
correct—"

"And *useful*," Cale interjected.

"—and useful," Tek agreed, "I want to turn the technique over to more capable people to implement it. This

is going to require thousands of workers and overseers, managers, engineers, all sorts of Vusstrans. I'm not an administrator."

Iji climbed down from detaching her comfortable lounge-nest that had hung from hooks and pulleys attached to the ceiling. "Sounds like you need to go off to a group school yourself." She grabbed a multitool and scrambled back up to begin dismantling the hardware mounted to the cermet structural beams.

Tek blinked, and then his broad lips curved in a smile. "Hmm, yes. That might be the answer. The Vusstran government wants to put me in charge of the worldwide restoration project, and I'm afraid I'd fail miserably. I'm much more of a person-to-person sort, just a simple scientist." He looked relieved. "I believe I need to take Cale away from here, to continue his education as well."

Cale worked at folding up Iji's bulky lounge-nest, making a show of how difficult the process was. "Well, I'm not going back to another Drifter colony, so you can just put that idea out of your head." He frowned at his work, then unrolled the lounge-nest with a sigh of disgust. "This ratty old thing is as ugly as it is clumsy, Ijit."

Iji looked down from the ceiling, where she had not yet disconnected a single one of the stability hooks. "Do it right, Cale. When I get to the group school, I'll have to mount everything all by myself."

"Poor baby," Cale said with a teasing grin, already imagining how she would react when she saw the present he had made for her in secret.

Tek looked at his foster son seriously. "Then we shall have to find a compromise, Cale. You must go to a place where you can learn to interact with Humans. And I'm coming with you."

With his father's ring firmly back on his hand, Cale had, for the first time in his life, actually set goals for himself. Remembering his fight with Klegg, Cale began lifting weights and using tension and resistance bands to build up his arms, shoulders, legs, and torso. He could already lift a squealing Iji over his head. He never wanted to feel like a weakling again. He also studied several biographies from Tek's library of individuals who had excelled in both negotiation and self-defense techniques.

He had decided to continue his education on technology and machinery in every possible form. It was an inborn skill, one of the few things Sam Tucker had given him.

"How about Tau-14?" Cale suggested, remembering the bustle and strangeness of the big asteroid. At least he knew there wouldn't be *too* many Humans at the station. "Can we get a job at the salvage yards?" Low life worms like Klegg probably only came through occasionally. And besides, the food had been pretty good.

Tek tapped his chin with one of his clawed fingers. "Hmm, perhaps. That might be a good solution. And it would be far enough from Vusstra that I could spend time with you, rather than being burdened by administrative details."

Hiding his smile of satisfaction, Cale crumpled up the lounge-nest, with exaggerated, mock-frustration. Iji let one of the hooks drop with a clatter from the ceiling, and cermet dust powdered her face. "Cale, be careful with that."

"Let's get the Ijit's cycle-day presents," Cale said. "I need a break from this mess anyway."

In the common room of the dwelling, the little pod-daughter was delighted to receive a high-yield, portable communicator, state-of-the-art in Vusstran science, from Tek. In fact, he'd had to go to the Vusstran government for a special license so that a child could own such a powerful and useful device.

"Now you can keep in touch with us, no matter where we go," Tek said, "though I had to get you appointed as an official part-time liaison with me." His skin discolored with embarrassment. "After that successful test, the Vusstran cabinet approves just about everything I ask for."

Iji tore open the overlarge present from Cale with even greater enthusiasm. "My most useful invention yet," he said, crossing his arms over his chest.

"And does it work?" Iji said before she had even seen what it was. Then she squealed to see a new lounge-nest, far more colorful and streamlined than the old one she had dismantled from her room.

"It's self-erecting, so you can pop it up anywhere in a second. No hassle," Cale explained. "I also included a low-grav generator, so you'll feel like you're floating all the time."

She hugged them both for their gifts. "I already feel like I'm floating."

At last, with relief and a little trepidation, Cale and Tek took off in the *Sword Ring*, headed toward Tau-14. Cale knew it was just his imagination as he peered through the cockpit windowports, but the weary, polluted world already looked a little greener. . . .

The government had been disheartened to see Tek depart, though they had extracted his promise that he would return a few times each cycle to oversee the progress of the environmental restoration. Also, when he felt his obligations to Cale had been completed, Tek agreed to return to Vusstra to take charge of the project, which would continue for decacycles to come.

The day before, he and Cale had accompanied Iji to group school and had seen her safely installed in the social pod to which she'd been assigned. The group pod's specialty (Iji's choice) would be environmental remediation through technology. Far from being apprehensive or depressed about the parting, Iji seemed filled with anticipation for this new stage in her life.

After demanding repeated promises to stay in touch via communicator, Iji hugged each of them goodbye. First her pod-father. "You ought to practice writing some of those biographies you like, Father. You may just have to write a book about me someday."

Then she turned to Cale. "Just wait. It won't be long before I'll be a great inventor like our father. And like your father—and you."

He flushed with embarrassment, but luckily his Vusstran family hadn't learned to interpret such subtleties of Human emotion.

A few months later, Tek sat observing Cale thoughtfully in the mess hall of the salvage station as they took their "evening meal" together. Cale fidgeted with the ring on his finger and used his food-rake to push his meal around the platter that sat in front of him. He had settled in rapidly, getting used to the daily work and the strangeness of Tau-14.

"I thought you liked Cook's Birstwittle Surprise," Tek said, indicating the pile of quivering nourishment on Cale's tray.

"Now that I've learned what Caldoch droppings taste like, some of the recipes have lost their charm." Cale shrugged. "I'm guessing the grav generator went out again while he was cooking. When that happens, everything in the kitchen starts floating around and, uh, weird stuff tends to get into the food. I think even Cook is surprised by the flavors when that happens."

Tek ate his own portion, pleasantly weary from a long day of study and calculations and lengthy transmissions between Tau-14 and Vusstra. He was still amazed at how well everything had worked out. Cale had easily gotten a job on an alternating-shift dismantling crew. His strength, agility, and knowledge of machinery grew steadily, though he still kept his distance from any Human coworkers. Rather than forming close friendships, as Tek had hoped, Cale seemed more often to be in competition with them.

Toying with his food-rake, Cale considered. "I'll have to take a look at that grav generator someday. Think I could fix it?"

"Patience and persistence," Tek said, looking meaningfully at the tattoo on Cale's upper arm. "Learn solidarity first. The rest will come."

He had sent out feelers and still hoped to make solid contact with some of the Humans who had worked closely with Sam Tucker on the Titan Project. Tek had done his best for years with the young man, but Cale needed something more than the Vusstran scientist could give him. For now, Tek was juggling his promises to Sam Tucker, and to Iji, and to the Vusstran government, and to the Qu'utians, and to Cale. Tek always kept his promises.

On his platter, Cale's food pulsed and congealed. "I think Cook's outdone himself this time." The Birstwittle Surprise responded by splattering a glob of sauce across the young man's cheek. "Hey!" He wiped his face. "All right, I was giving you the benefit of the doubt, but you're *provoking* me into eating you."

"Cale, don't play with your food—and don't talk to it, either," Tek said.

Tek watched Cale rake down several forkfuls of the food and smack his lips with relish. As his hands moved, Sam Tucker's gold ring glinted in the light of the mess hall.

Someday, Tek thought.

The boy still had no idea of how much promise he held within himself.

Even before they met, they affected each other's destiny! Get the whole story of their tumultuous formative years. Don't miss *Titan A.E.: Akima's Story*, also in paperback from Ace books.